12-98

DS

PEACEMAKER
BOUNTY

PEACEMAKER
BOUNTY

•

CLIFFORD BLAIR

AVALON BOOKS
THOMAS BOUREGY AND COMPANY, INC.
401 LAFAYETTE STREET
NEW YORK, NEW YORK 10003

PRINTED IN THE UNITED STATES OF AMERICA
ON ACID-FREE PAPER
BY HADDON CRAFTSMEN, BLOOMSBURG, PENNSYLVANIA

With love,
to Donald and Helen McAnally,
Uncle Donald and Aunt Helen:
friends, relatives,
and fellow believers.

Chapter One

"Jim!" a woman's familiar voice called over the bustle of the crowd, then switched quickly to the longer, more formal version of his name: "James!"

Startled, Stark turned. The suitcase in his hand made him a little awkward in the press of disembarking passengers on the depot platform. They were the usual mix of businessmen, ranchers, family groups, and drummers.

Eagerly, he scanned their ranks. Beside him, the train cut loose with its ear-splitting whistle, drowning any further calls. But in a moment he spotted the welcome feminine form moving with hurried grace through the crowd toward him.

It had been nigh onto four weeks since he'd laid eyes on Prudence McKay's petite shape, and Stark was a little surprised at how much pleasure he took from seeing her hurry breathlessly up to him.

She looked just as pleasing as he remembered, with her lovely features flushed just a little from her exertions. Her dark hair was done stylishly in cascading ringlets and curls. A frilled blue dress displayed her attractive figure in modest fashion. Not for the first time, Stark thought that she hardly looked the part of the savvy attorney and counselor at law she actually was.

Automatically he put down his suitcase, then hesi-

1

tated, not sure what he'd do once he had his hands empty. Embracing her in greeting was surely out of the question. There was nothing but friendship between them, of course, he reminded himself. And heaven help the poor hombre who tried to tame this headstrong filly.

But still, he felt like he ought to do something. . . .

Oddly, Prudence too seemed at loose ends now that she had caught up with him. She moved her dainty feet in an uncertain little dance, then reached impulsively to touch his chest with a gesture that was part affection and part restraint. She had touched him like that before. Resolutely, then, she lowered her hands to her sides and stood stiffly. Her cheeks were bright red.

"How was New York?" she spoke all in a rush.

"Big and crowded," Stark said hoarsely. "It's good to be back." He realized he didn't want to take his eyes off her, and made himself look quickly away. He figured his face was flushing as much as hers now.

At the invite of his old employers, reinforced with their offer of a hefty fee, he had spent the last three weeks teaching the ropes of Western law enforcement to new Pinkerton operatives slated to man various of the detective agency's offices in lesser developed parts of the country. It *was* good to be back to more familiar stomping grounds. Prudence being there to greet him made it even better.

"Evett Nix said he needed to see you," she explained. "I remembered you were returning today, and told him I'd come by and meet you after I closed the office."

Remotely, it occurred to Stark that she must've stopped at her hotel suite to change from her usual, more austere office attire. There were little blue ribbons, lighter than the rest of the fabric, adorning the shallow neckline of her dress, he noted, then caught himself as her words sank in.

"Evett wants to see me?" he probed.

Prudence gave a quick nod, then anticipated his next question, as she was wont to do. "He didn't say why. But he seemed to think it was important."

U.S. Marshal Evett Nix ramrodded the formidable ranks of federal lawmen in Oklahoma Territory. In his trade, Stark did his best to stay in the good graces of the marshal. It wasn't always easy to do.

"Reckon I'll go ahead and swing by his office right now," he decided aloud. "Don't want to keep the man waiting."

"It's on my way. I'll go with you," Prudence announced.

Stark offered his arm.

"Peacemaker!" a man shouted.

Stark knew the tone, recognized the strident challenge in it. He'd heard it all too often before, over the years of riding the trouble trail. Another gunwolf looking to carve a notch, representing James Stark, in the butt of his six-gun. His rep as a fast gun and freelance troubleshooter working on the side of law and order had made him a target of more such challenges than he cared to remember.

Stark was turning smoothly, easing Prudence aside, brushing back the tail of his corduroy coat to clear the way to his Colt—the single-action .45 that gave him his sobriquet—before the challenge had finished sounding.

He found himself facing a crouching figure with arms

crooked to hover over holstered pistols, as the crowd parted between them. Amateur's stance, he thought, but some old pros were good enough to make it work for them. He didn't recognize his challenger, who was just another face in the late afternoon light.

Prudence was well clear. He had a side view of her pale, stricken features. "There's no need for this," he called, to try to stop what was coming.

He never got a chance to say more. "Dead or alive, Stark! Slap iron!"

Stark drew. He didn't know his foe, so he made it fast, snapping the Colt up and firing with a single blurred flick of his wrist, his body straight as a fence post.

The crouching figure convulsed, guns half drawn. He hadn't needed to draw so fast after all, Stark realized. One slug should be enough. Coolly, bitterly, he shot again, in case he was wrong. Both guns clattered unfired to the boards of the platform as their owner crumpled.

Stark looked sharply left and right, the smoking Colt still level in his fist. He saw nothing to alarm him among the gaping spectators. With mechanical precision he ejected the empties and reloaded.

He felt some of the stiffness leave his face as he shifted his eyes to Prudence. The earlier flush was entirely gone from her features. She was pale and wide-eyed. Her full lips parted to speak.

Stark plucked up his suitcase and reached her in a stride. He caught her elbow and steered her through the ranks of onlookers. "Come on."

"But the law—" she protested.

"We're going to the marshal's office," Stark reminded her tersely. "We'll report it there."

She yielded, and he shepherded her down the steps off the platform. No one offered a protest. Behind them, the murmur of voices began to rise.

After a moment she shrugged sharply against his grip, and he released her. She hurried to match his swift pace, and he glimpsed the anxious sideward glance she cast up at his profile.

A bleak anger rode him. What a homecoming, he thought savagely. He'd had to kill some tenderfoot, and, worse, in a sense, Prudence had been there to witness it. He knew it was the violent side of him that she found so hard to tolerate.

"Sorry you had to see that," he muttered gruffly without looking at her.

She actually missed a step. "What?" she gasped.

"Forget it." Stark slowed his step to accommodate her.

"That shooting wasn't your fault," she declared with surprising fervor. "You didn't have a choice. He forced you into drawing."

Stark felt a sense of bemusement. Usually Prudence was quick to condemn the killing that was one of the trappings of his profession. "Durned fool, pulling on me that way," he said under his breath. He knew from the way the gunwolf had fallen that he was dead.

They were passing by the ornate Victorian architecture of Guthrie's downtown. There was quite a bit of mounted and pedestrian traffic as the business day drew to a close. His nerves still thrumming, Stark glanced back. He frowned at the somehow vaguely familiar figure of a horseman about a block behind them.

The ratcheting double click of the lever action on a repeating rifle gave him a half-second's warning. No time to be gentle this go-around. He dropped his suitcase and shoved Prudence hard aside. He heard her startled cry, glimpsed the swirl of her blue dress, as he wheeled and dropped to one knee. His gun came up and out, even faster than it did against the gunwolf, because this time he figured he was going up against a dead drop.

Flame spiked from the shadows of an alley across the street; a slug ripped overhead. Stark cocked and triggered the Colt three times, firing as fast the bullets would fly, raking the narrow mouth of the alley with gunfire.

He heard a scream and saw a figure lurch into view. In the same heartbeat, shots rang out and echoed from down the street behind him. He dived into a roll, feeling the bruising hardness of the cobblestones beneath his shoulder. He came out of it flat on his belly, head whirling, but with the Colt held steady at the end of an outstretched arm.

Folks were scattering. The horseman he'd glimpsed was reining his prancing mount. A motionless figure lay sprawled almost beneath the animal's hooves. As Stark watched, the rider thrust a pistol downward and fired a second time. The prone form jerked, then lay still again. A safety shot—the brand of a cold-blooded professional.

And suddenly Stark knew why the man who'd likely saved his life had looked familiar.

Stark clambered to his feet. The horseman gave a last appraising glance at his victim, then came cantering toward him. Stark spared a look at Prudence. Wisely, she had stayed down. He made no move to give her a hand. He wasn't for-sure certain that the trouble was over.

The horseman reined up his prancing steeldust gelding a couple of yards distant. Deliberately, he holstered his Colt revolver—nearly a twin of Stark's own.

"Sorry bronc still needs some work if he's going to spook at a little bit of gunplay," the rider declared. "Had my last one trained where he'd stand rock steady during a dustup like that. Lost him when some sorry cuss tried to turn the tables and dry-gulch me. The bounty on him covered this new Cayuse, and left me a bit of spending money." He gave a rueful shake of his head. "Just have to work with this one a little more." Then he grinned engagingly from beneath his full mustache. "Looks like you owe me one, Peacemaker."

Stark returned his own gun to leather, squinting up to study the lean, square-jawed face. "Appears that way, don't it, Gundance?" he drawled easily.

"I'd say it does. Who's the pretty lady?" He cast an admiring gaze on Prudence as she rose easily to her feet, brushing dust from her dress.

Still keeping an eye cocked in his direction, Stark moved closer to Prudence. He gave her a quick, inquiring glance. Even a bit disheveled, she was lovely. She had been studying the the newcomer with wide eyes, but she broke it off to give Stark a quick, reassuring nod.

"Prudence McKay, meet Lance Trowbridge," Stark said dryly. "Also known in some circles as Gundance."

"Pleased, I'm sure," Prudence spoke without inflection. She swayed a little closer to Stark.

"Miss McKay is one of the territory's few lady attorneys," Stark added.

Trowbridge looked impressed. "An attorney who is a beautiful woman as well. I *am* honored, Miss McKay." Left-handed, he doffed his Stetson with a sweeping gesture.

"What ill wind blows you to these parts?" Stark queried.

"Just passing through on my way to the Indian Lands," Gundance answered almost lazily. "Saw that little fracas back at the depot. Nice shooting, by the way. Then I saw these two rannies tracking you, and decided they might be up to no good. I was right. I declare, Peacemaker, it sure does seem to be open season on you today."

Stark had the same unsettling notion. What in blazes was going on? he asked himself. Three men had tried to kill him in not much over a quarter of an hour. He was used to violence, used to stepping wary, used to challenges from ambitious gun toughs. But this stampede of killers on his tail was enough to set even *his* teeth on edge.

He used his chin to indicate Gundance's victim and the curious onlookers beginning to cluster around like vultures. "Who was he?"

Gundance shrugged broad shoulders that were all bone and rawhide. "Some no-account hardcase from up in No-Man's-Land. Seen him around, but don't recollect his handle. Doesn't matter much nohow; ain't no price on his head. More's the pity. I might've picked up a few greenbacks while saving your hide." The dangerous, easygoing grin flashed.

A crowd was beginning to gather around them. Stark heard a murmur that the rifleman in the alley was dead. Wordlessly, he legged it across the street, the spectators drawing hastily clear. Prudence hung back only a little. Gundance walked his gray delicately over the brick paving stones.

Stark stared down into the slack face of a hard-bitten stranger. He glanced inquisitively up at Gundance.

Trowbridge shrugged again. "Search me. Another fair piece of shooting, though."

Stark shook his head in bafflement. This pair hadn't even bothered with a challenge. They'd been after his scalp, plain and simple. Trying to settle some real or fancied grudge, he supposed. He wondered if they'd figured it was worth their lives. He sensed Prudence's troubled gaze on him.

"Believe I'll be moving on," Trowbridge said, disturbing his reverie. "You'll square things with the authorities, I trust? Law dogs never cotton much to me, which I surely don't understand, seeing as how I'm only giving them a hand doing their job."

"Maybe if you brought a wanted man in alive once in a while, they'd see things a little different," Stark suggested wryly.

Gundance hitched his shoulders. "Fair fights all. Wouldn't kill a man without first giving him a chance to draw against me."

In most cases a chance to pull a gun against a pistolero of Trowbridge's caliber could hardly be called a fair fight, but Stark didn't speak the thought aloud. "Hit the trail," he said. "I'll see this isn't held to your account."

"Obliged, Peacemaker. Watch your back. Next time I might not be there to cover it." His grin had a twist to it. He sketched a salute at Prudence. "So long, Miss McKay."

Prudence's nod of acknowledgment was little more than a dip of her chin.

Gundance's grin grew wider. He urged the gray into a canter that scattered the growing throng of onlookers as he passed through their ranks. Stark saw him glance back once with a keenly gauging eye. Gundance was taking his own advice. He was watching his back.

Prudence drew closer to Stark's side. "That was him? The bounty hunter everybody talks about?"

"Yep." Stark continued to observe his silhouetted figure.

Prudence sniffed disdainfully. "Well, I can certainly see how he might talk men into giving themselves up."

Stark shook his head. "Not his style. The only talking he does is before he pulls his gun."

Chapter Two

"Plenty of witnesses saw both incidents," U.S. Marshal Evett Nix advised. "Several of them saw Trowbridge warn the second gunman before he threw down on him. Trowbridge didn't even pull his gun until the hombre turned on him, with a rifle already in his hands. Then Trowbridge shot him dead." Reluctant respect edged the lawman's tones.

"Shot him dead twice," Stark added.

"Yeah." Nix leaned back in his leather swivel chair behind the broad expanse of his desk. It was all but covered with tidy stacks of files and paperwork. The neatness reflected Nix's background as a successful businessman before he'd been appointed U.S. Marshal of Oklahoma Territory.

Here in his office in the Herriott Building, attired in a natty suit, with his handlebar mustache carefully trimmed, he still had the look of a businessman. But, Stark was willing to admit, Nix had come into his own ramrodding the small army of deputies he'd recruited to serve under him. All were willing to take his orders, although many, such as stalwarts Heck Thomas, Bill Tilghman, and Chris Madsen, had far more experience in the field. That said something about Nix's character and strength of will.

The lawman frowned broodingly, as if musing over his next words. His eyes shifted from Stark to Prudence, seated beside the troubleshooter in front of the desk. "Trowbridge is bad medicine," he contented himself with saying.

Stark's mouth quirked. "To hear him tell it, he's just giving you a little assist in doing your job."

"Oh, he brings in more wanted men than any bounty tracker out there," Nix conceded. "Even more than you, James. Difference is, he brings them all in dead. That sticks in my craw."

"Then all the stories about him are true?" Prudence queried. "Even if a man wants to surrender, he forces him into a shoot-out?"

Nix nodded soberly. "I reckon it's true enough. And he's never lost, despite having gone up against some mighty fast gunhands. No telling how many notches he could carve on his pistol butt if he was of a mind to."

"How did he get that awful sobriquet, Gundance?" Prudence persisted.

"Story is, he kept shooting a man after he'd nailed him dead center," Stark answered her. "The impacts of the bullets held the fellow on his feet a couple of seconds longer than otherwise. Trowbridge said he liked the way the bullets made him jump. Called it the gundance. Some wag tacked the name onto him and it's stuck ever since."

Prudence shuddered visibly.

"I know for a fact that a lot of the bodies he brings in have more than enough lead in them to get the job done," Nix said grimly. "Gundance is a man-killer, right enough. He's the top bounty hunter in the country, so far as I know, and one of the most dangerous men alive with a gun.''

"More dangerous than Jim?'' Prudence demanded, then looked surprised she'd asked the question.

Nix remained silent.

"So it's been said,'' Stark murmured.

"I think his presence and the attempts on your life today might all be tied together,'' Nix said deliberately.

Stark straightened in his chair. "How's that?''

Nix hesitated, then cleared his throat diplomatically. "This may be on the order of a personal matter.'' His eyes shuttled from Stark to Prudence.

"Whatever's going on put Prudence in the line of fire,'' Stark stated firmly. "She's already involved. She has a right to be here. Besides, she's my . . . legal counsel.''

Nix blinked. Prudence's hazel eyes touched Stark in a way that was oddly warm and intimate.

Prudence had actually represented him on at least one occasion. And, Stark realized, he really did value her insight on this mystery. He felt a sense of surprise. He was used to relying on no one but himself.

"Very well.'' Nix opened a desk drawer, extracted a tattered sheet of paper folded in quarters, and carefully straightened it out. Then he poked it across the desk.

Stark took it as Prudence leaned closer to see. He heard her gasp and was barely aware of her rising to stand close behind him and peer over his shoulder for a better view.

Printed words jumped out at him. WANTED . . . DEAD . . . JAMES STARK, THE PEACEMAKER.

Below the boldface block capital letters was a crude

sketch of a man's face. It could have been his own. Pretty clearly, it was meant to be.

Under the picture was the figure $5,000. A small line of print read, "Proof of death required—Deliver to Indian Territory." There was nothing else on the poster.

An eerie feeling touched Stark. How many other men's names and pictures had he eyeballed on similiar fliers? "At least I don't come cheap," he commented dryly.

"Where did you get this?" Prudence demanded.

"They started showing up about a week ago," Nix replied. "Word is, they're spread pretty thick around the Indian Lands and in the border towns on Hell's Fringe."

"Somebody sure wants my hide," Stark said. He was having a little trouble taking this seriously, but three dead men on the streets of Guthrie were enough to tell him that some folks were taking it mighty serious indeed.

"We don't know who's behind it," Nix went on, "but I've got my men checking things out. I wanted to let you know as soon as you hit town so you could lay low." He missed Stark's frown. "I didn't move quite fast enough. My apologies for exposing you to danger, Miss McKay."

"Never mind any threat to me." Prudence brushed Nix's contrition aside. "This must be someone who has a grudge against Jim."

"Granted," Nix agreed. "Any ideas, James?"

Stark mulled it over. He'd piled up plenty of enemies over the years, but this didn't smack of any that came readily to mind. He shook his head ruefully. "Nope."

"It probably stems from something that happened relatively recently," Prudence prompted.

Stark squelched a surprising spark of irritation. "I've been out of the territorries for a month. And it was six weeks ago that I brought in those three stage robbers."

"None of them were wanted," Nix recollected. "Apparently the stage holdup was a first job. They fouled it up."

They'd fouled it up worse when they'd tried to bushwhack him and forced his play, Stark reflected sourly. His retainer with the stage line had set him on their trail. He'd brought them in dead, rather than alive.

"A drifter identified the third from the newspaper picture," Nix added. "Tagged him as Marty Kincaid from the Indian Lands. Didn't know anything else about him."

Prudence took the circular from Stark. Her soft hand brushed his. "How would someone go about collecting?"

"They're saying that whoever posted this has ways of finding out if the reward is due, and that it wouldn't be a good idea to try to collect under false pretenses. Folks aren't willing to share much with my deputies. But the outlaws obviously know enough to take the offer seriously. Anyone who earns it will likely know how to go about collecting."

"But if the bounty is real, why did Lance Trowbridge interfere when those men were to trying to kill you?" Prudence asked Stark suddenly.

"Because he didn't want to share the reward," Nix suggested.

Stark shook his head. "Gundance wouldn't go up

against me for a paltry five thousand dollars. The risk is too great that I'd beat him. He'd want more.''

"Well, a lot of other hombres will be willing to try,'' Nix predicted darkly.

"I know,'' Stark agreed. ''And I can't afford to wait around for your boys to get to the bottom of it. Come morning, I'll be heading across Hell's Fringe into Indian Territory. I'll root out whoever's behind this and cancel the bounty my own way.''

"Jim, that's foolish!'' Prudence snapped sharply.

Stark regarded her for a long brooding moment. ''If I want your advice, counselor,'' he said coldly, ''I'll ask for it.''

Prudence's eyes blazed. ''Excuse me, Mr. Stark, I thought you had done just that.''

"She's got a point, James,'' Nix cut in. ''Once you hit the trail you'll have every two-bit gunslick, hardcase, and bounty hunter in two territories looking to get you in their sights and earn that bounty.''

"Earning it won't come easy.''

Nix gave a disgusted snort. ''You're like a lightning rod right now. I can't stop you going where you please, but I won't be responsible for protecting you if you won't cooperate with me. And I won't have your mere presence provoking gunfights in this city. Is that understood?''

Stark nodded. He couldn't blame Nix for his attitude. ''I'll do my own protecting.''

Prudence rose abruptly. ''If you gentlemen will pardon me, I have other matters to attend to,'' she announced without looking at Stark.

"I'll see you home,'' Stark said gruffly as he rose.

"Don't bother."

But she made no objection as he accompanied her along the streets to the hotel where she lodged, although she maintained a consistent distance between them. Her back was as rigid as a fireplace poker, and she didn't speak.

Stark wondered sourly what had happened to his earlier eagerness to have her advice and counsel. As always, her high-handed ways had gotten his back up.

He kept his eyes open, but no lurking gunmen or bushwhackers accosted them. At the door to her suite, she used her key, and for a moment he thought she would go inside without acknowledging him at all. Then her shoulders slumped slightly and she turned back to face him. He hadn't realized that he'd moved closer to her. Her sweet scent teased his nostrils. She had to look up into his face.

"Jim," she implored softly, "please be reasonable about this. At least give Evett a few days to try to get it straightened out. . . ."

She broke off as he stepped back a bit. "Whatever I do, they're bound to keep coming," he pointed out, trying to be reasonable himself. "I won't turn tail, I won't go into hiding, and I won't sit and wait for them. If I'm going to be a target, I'm going to be the one that's closing in on the hombre who's behind all this. That's the only way to settle it."

"Evett and his deputies will settle it eventually," she persisted.

Stark snorted. "Their hands are all but tied in Indian Territory unless they have specific federal charges they can bring. I don't have to tell you the law. Even if they do get it settled, it may not be before I make a slip, or some yahoo gets lucky, and the bounty gets paid. A man in my line of work, with my reputation, can't afford to sit tight. I've got to strike back.''

"So is that what this is all about?" she demanded with a trace of fire, "your reputation as a gunman?"

"My reputation, my profession. Call it what you will. If I let this go unchallenged, word will get out that I've lost my nerve, and then things will get even worse. I really will be a target then. And no one would hire me."

"Would that be so bad?" she murmured, her eyes bright, before wheeling away from him. With her slender back to him, she went on, "Jim, why do you keep on making your living this way? You're a decent, God-fearing man. I just can't understand how you can justify hiring out your gun. I've tried; honestly I have. But I just don't understand."

He wanted to reach and touch her, but her unyielding figure stayed his hand. He groped for words.

" 'Blessed be the Lord my strength,' " he quoted then, " 'Which teacheth my hands to war, and my fingers to fight.' That's Scripture, and it pretty much describes me; it's my gift, if you want to call it that. Whatever else I can or can't do, I can fight; I can make war. And I'm fighting a kind of war against the breed of men who'd overrun this territory if they had the chance. Sure, I get paid for using my gun, but I won't work for just anybody who offers me money. I choose what causes I'm going to fight for. You know that."

He broke off, aware he'd been starting to sound like some circuit preacher. But he did his preaching with a gun, and Prudence McKay was too good and virtuous a woman to ever fully accept that—too good for him; that was for certain.

So why was it so consarned important that he justify himself to her?

Wordlessly, he turned to leave her. She must've sensed his movement. He thought she made a small sound that was almost a moan. Then she whirled suddenly and flung herself against him, her arms closing so tightly they cut off his breath. She buried her face against his chest.

"Be careful." He caught her muffled whisper. "Come home to me!" He wasn't sure about the last words.

All in a clock-tick of time, before he could react, she released him, spun like a prairie antelope, and slipped into her room. The door closed firmly in her wake.

Nonplussed, Stark stood staring at the panel. He started to reach for the knob, then stopped. What had gotten into her? From an angry lecture, to an embrace that left him gasping. He felt stirrings that he quickly tamped back down. He'd never figure the woman out. He'd be a fool to dwell on the sorts of notions he'd been having about her lately.

While he'd been back East, he'd missed her mightily, he had to admit, but she was too headstrong and set in her ways to ever change.

Just like him.

Scowling, he stalked back down the stairs and passed through the lobby, ignoring the nod from the clerk. Fool ought to mind his own business, he groused to himself.

He was sure there'd be paperwork to clear up at his office, so he headed in that direction. He wanted to be ready to leave in the morning before the town got to stirring.

Cautious, he stayed in the shadows, avoiding the pools of light cast by the gas street lamps. No telling how many other hardcases might be looking to carry proof of his death back to their mysterious benefactor in Indian Territory.

The mouth of an alley gaped on his right. He trod lightly past it, casting his eyes sideward, which was the best way for seeing at night.

Movement startled him. A figure lurched out of the darkness. Stark drew and cocked and froze his finger in the last piece of a heartbeat before he dropped the hammer.

"Wait, mister!" a voice, shocked into soberness, gasped. The disheveled figure of what had to be an Eastern drummer, derby hat askew, staggered to a halt. The whites of his eyes were wide in the darkness.

"Just been over to the saloon," he babbled. "Reckon I lost my way."

"Stay out of mine," Stark growled.

He moved on by, keeping the Colt leveled on the befuddled fellow. The drunkenness could've all been an act.

Stark's palm was sweaty when he holstered the Peacemaker. Nix had been right, he reflected grimly. His enemies were legion. When he crossed the border into the Indian Lands every man's hand would be turned against him.

Another fragment of Scripture crossed his mind: "The son of man hath not where to lay his head."

Chapter Three

At dusk, Stark rode into the border town of Purcell. He'd been traveling mostly at night, avoiding settlements and any other signs of humanity he had seen. The distant wink of a campfire had been a signal to swing wide to bypass whoever bedded down by its flames. He was always wary when he was on the trail, but a new caution had been bred in him these past days.

He had forded the south fork of the Canadian River into the Chickasaw Nation, doubling back to ride into Purcell as if emerging from the Indian Lands. If anybody was waiting for him, they likely wouldn't expect him to be coming from the west.

Few of the horsemen or townsfolk paid much heed to him as he drifted his big sorrel through town. In a dark tan duster, with a growth of beard fringing his jaw, he looked to be just another saddle tramp.

Only a few of the old hands might've noticed that he was a little better armed than most drifters. His namesake Colt .45 revolver rode at his waist, along with his sheathed bowie. His .38 Marlin double-action hideout gun was tucked snugly behind his gun belt at the small of his back. The butts of two Winchester saddle guns jutted from their sheaths, ready to hand. On his right

was the 1887 lever-action shotgun; on his left, the long-range 1886 Sporting Rifle.

There was no need for all that armament at the moment. Purcell was a reputable enough town these days, presided over by U.S. Deputies Bill Carr and John Swain. Built in anticipation of the coming of the Atchison, Topeka and Santa Fe Railroad into Indian Territory, and named after the line's local director, Purcell had thrived when the rails finally came through.

A center for the commerce and trade passing back and forth between the Indian Lands and Oklahoma Territory, the town boasted churches, schools, a variety of stores, meat markets, competing blacksmiths, a livery, and even a mammoth icehouse.

Stark rode past the balconied front of the ornate Love Hotel as he headed toward the river he had crossed outside of town. Purcell was peaceable enough today, but Stark had heard the old-timers tell of being nigh able to read a newspaper at midnight from the constant flash of gunfire in the town's rambunctious youth. And there was still a part of town where that sort of lawless spirit held sway.

Stark was headed there now.

The street dropped steeply away as it led down to the river bottoms, and the buildings became more disreputable and shabby. On the far side of the river was Oklahoma Territory, where selling liquor was legal. Over here, in the Indian Lands, it was not. The motley collection of tents, shacks, and saloons known as Sand Bar Town had been spawned to meet the sordid trade in alcohol and sin that had developed along with the more legitimate types of commerce.

Situated on an unstable sandbar in the river, the community catered to whiskey peddlers, hardcases, card sharps, and thirsty hombres from both territories, as well as a few of the better citizens of Purcell. The local deputies rarely set foot there, and then only at the risk of their lives. Sand Bar Town was a tiny no-man's-land, where the law was written by the fastest and the steadiest gun. And, unless Stark missed his guess, from its sorry denizens he'd find out how a fellow could go about collecting the bounty posted on the Peacemaker.

He dismounted at the hitching rail at the water's edge and looked out across the darkening river. An early moon was casting a faint glint from its silvered surface. This was normally a shallow ford, but the current could run deceptively fast. Spring rains had swollen it in the past few weeks. Clutching pools of quicksand waited for the boot of the careless.

A rickety wooden boardwalk extended out over the water. At its end, some fifty yards out, Stark could see the lights of Sand Bar Town's most infamous establishment, the saloon known as the Ark. The name was apt, after a fashion. Built on wooden stakes driven deep into the river bottom, the Ark resembled nothing so much as a huge wooden crate. Once, when swept away by floodwaters, it had floated downriver and finally washed ashore. When found, it had been towed back and set once more in place. It reopened for business only a little the worse for wear, serving a cosmopolitan mix of townsfolk and lowlifes.

Stark glanced about. His only company consisted of the horses at the hitch rail. Satisfied, he took a few moments to make his arrangements. Then, moving his stiff right leg in a swinging limp, he ventured out onto the boardwalk.

His awkward gait didn't make the crossing any easier. There were no handrails or lights, and the twelve-inch boards underfoot had been so warped by time and weather that some of them were curled up at the ends. They shifted alarmingly under his weight. The dark water raced past a yard beneath his boots. More than one drunken yahoo, returning from the saloon, had lost his balance and toppled into the river. A few of them had never come out.

Gratefully, Stark hobbled at last onto the platform serving as the structure's porch. The boxlike building loomed close beside him. In the poor light, only a faint hint of the walls' garish yellow paint was visible.

He tugged the brim of his Stetson down even tighter over his brow, let his shoulders sag like those of a stove-up bronc rider, and pushed into the Ark. Absent a close inspection, he doubted anybody would be able to recognize him as the wanted Peacemaker.

The dim, smoky interior of the Ark didn't lend itself to close inspection of much of anything, from the card games, to the painted faces of the floozies, to the labels on the bottles of cheap whiskey. Stark got out of the doorway and took a handful of seconds to get the lay of the land. Nothing much had changed. A few heads turned his way, but his entry didn't stir up any great interest. Just one more drifter looking to cut the dust in his throat. The fanciest thing in the place was the hand-carved mahogany piano on a low stage beside the bar. The tinny notes drifted up to be absorbed by the muffling smoke hanging overhead.

Stark limped the length of the bar. This was the first time he'd been in close human company for a couple of days, and the nearness of so many possible enemies made his neck prickle, like a centipede was walking across it. At any moment he expected to feel its sting.

Keeping his head down, he eyed the men he passed. A few were familiar. He spotted the unlikely tableful of lawyers who often came here to discuss the day's cases in the local court.

A lean lath of an hombre had his shoulders propped against the far wall, a near-empty bottle dangling in a knobby fist. From his leathery face, to his fur cap, to his Sharps Big Fifty rifle, to the fighting knife at his side, he had the look of an old-time frontiersman. Even from a distance, he stank of wolves. The skull of one of the beasts dangled from a rope around his lean waist, like some grisly charm. A wolfer—a dying breed. His half-closed eyes stared blankly into the haze.

Stark stopped at the bar. The burly barkeep dropped the black iron hook that served as his right hand onto the bar with a thump. Hooky had lost that hand in a gunfight, Stark knew, but it hadn't made him any less dangerous of a man to cross. Up close, that hook could be as deadly as any gun. And Hooky had lost none of his gunman's speed.

"Beer," Stark muttered.

The barkeep eyed him, but didn't show any sign of recognition. There was nothing in this broken-down, bearded stranger to bring James Stark to mind. Wordlessly, he shoved a foaming mug across. Stark grunted, put down a coin, and turned away. As he did, his stiff right leg bumped against the bar. He glimpsed the barkeep's suddenly narrowed eyes and berated himself mentally as he hobbled to an empty corner table.

Seated, with his leg stretched out before him, the folds of the duster arranged over it, he observed the room with a hooded gaze as he took token sips of his beer. Hooky, he noted, was tending to another customer and no longer seemed interested in him.

Snatches and pieces of talk between the other patrons reached his ears. The lawyers were talking about a certain judge whose latest ruling none of them seemed to care for. A couple of cowhands were joshing one of the hired girls. She was playing along.

Then Stark stiffened as a familiar name reached him.

"I hear Lance Trowbridge is after him."

The remark came from one of a quartet of hardcases engaged in a low-stakes game of poker. Stark pricked up his ears, straining to hear.

One of the other players snorted. "If Gundance is after him, Stark won't stand a chance. Good riddance, I say!"

"I don't know about that. Stark's awful fast," another one offered. "I seen him take down a pistolero who challenged him over to Meridian. It was like he didn't even have to draw; that big Colt was just in his fist, spitting bullets."

Gundance will shade him," the bounty hunter's supporter said with assurance.

"Hanged if that wouldn't be something to see," the fourth member of the quarter spoke up. "The two fastest guns alive going up against each other! Not many of their kind left."

Stark shifted his stiffened leg and kept listening.

"My money's on Gundance," spoke up an hombre from a neighboring table. "Two to one."

"Let's see the money!" Stark's booster snapped. "I'll take that!"

"Three to one on Gundance!" another patron said, entering the bidding.

Stark let the wagering run its course. The odds were running two to one against him when it was over, he calculated bleakly. Even the lawyers had stopped their palaver to pay attention. The piano player was taking a break.

"Five thousand dollars," one of the first quartet of hardcases spoke musingly. "Wouldn't mind having that to keep me warm on the cold nights."

"You'd pay the devil collecting it!" one of his cohorts said, and earned a chorus of chuckles.

His comrade was undeterred. "Maybe so, but if I didn't have to go up against him face-to-face, I might be willing to risk it."

"Yeah, especially if you had two or three other guns siding you!"

"I reckon I'm big enough to share."

There was a murmur of agreement.

Stark eased his leg again beneath the duster, letting one hand rest lightly on his knee. "Just who is it that's offering this reward I been hearing about?" he said, to thrust himself gruffly into the conversation.

Eyes—some hostile, some curious—shifted to rest on him.

"What's it to you, stranger?" one hardcase challenged.

"Figured I might go about collecting it."

"Sure, you and what army, Peg Leg?"

"Don't need two good legs to pull a trigger," Stark drawled, and got a round of laughter of his own.

"Big shot by the name of Lucius Kincaid put that bounty up," one of the gamblers volunteered. "Millionaire from back East somewheres. Came here some years ago and built himself a goldarned fortress out in the Lands. Got a whole passel of gun hawks working for him."

Stark's mind clicked over like the cylinder revolving in a six-gun. "He good for that much *dinero?*" he queried, to buy a moment's time for ruminating.

"Shoot, he'd never miss it! And he ain't the type to renege, neither. Someone brings him Stark's carcass, and he'll pay off in gold coin!"

Several listeners muttered agreement. Stark didn't like having the whole room's attention focused on him, but there was no way around it at this juncture.

"What'd Stark do to get Kincaid so riled?" he asked, although he already knew the answer now.

"Killed his son—gunned him down."

"His boy an outlaw, was he?" Stark pressed on. "I hear the Peacemaker don't buck the law."

"It don't make no nevermind to Kincaid the whys and wherefores of how it happened. His boy's dead, and he aims to see Stark pay!"

"Kincaid's the one who'll pay," a wag offered. "To the tune of five thousand dollars to get Stark killed!"

"Couldn't happen to a more deserving fellow, either," another patron joined in. "Stark's just a fancy-dan gunslick who figures he's too good for the rest of us."

He didn't have very many supporters here, Stark concluded darkly. He figured he ought to put in two bits in his own defense. "Collecting that reward won't come easy," he opined loudly. "I hear Stark's sure death with just about any kind of lead thrower!"

"Thought you was going to bring him in, hopalong!"

"Reckon I may have reconsidered."

As they laughed, he levered himself to his feet. He had what he'd come for. No point in pushing his luck.

He began to thread his way awkwardly past the tables. He was halfway to the door when the barkeep called, "Hey, limpy!"

Stark stopped. "Yeah?"

Wordlessly, Hooky jerked his head for Stark to approach.

Stark hesitated. The less attention he drew to himself now, the better. But ignoring the Ark's proprietor would only make him more conspicuous.

Muttering, he lurched to the bar. "What do you want?"

Hooky ducked his head to peer more closely under the brim of Stark's Stetson. "You didn't pay me for that beer."

"Like fire I didn't—" Stark started to protest, then saw Hooky's ugly mouth twist in a triumphant snarl of recognition.

"It's him, boys!" he bawled. "The Peacemaker himself!" And he brought the black hook around in a vicious swipe at Stark's neck.

In that moment Hooky came blamed close to collecting the bounty. Stark snapped his left up like he was blocking a roundhouse punch in the ring, and felt the hardness of the barkeep's metal-sheathed stump strike bruisingly against his forearm. He swung his right fist in a savage swipe of his own, and his knuckles ground into the softness under Hooky's ear with a satisfying impact.

Hooky's shrewd eyes rolled up in his skull and he dropped like a trapdoor had opened under him. Left foot planted solidly, Stark wheeled toward the sudden uproar among the other patrons. As he turned, he swept his right hand down to rip the concealing drape of the duster aside.

Hands were already darting for holstered guns among the crowd. Even faster, Stark tore the lever-action shotgun loose from the hideout rig with which he'd strapped it to his leg. He swung the barrel up as his other hand ratcheted the lever.

"Don't try it, boys!" he roared. "Double-ought buckshot, and I'm sure death with it!"

The room froze as if it was an artist's painting with a half-dozen or more hardcases caught in various stages of rising or pulling iron. A chair crashed over backward, but nothing else moved. They could still likely take him, but a goodly portion of them would go down trying, and they knew it.

Stark could guess what had happened. When he'd accidentally bumped the concealed shotgun against the bar, Hooky must've noticed something out of place. His limited disguise had not been able to withstand the barkeep's skeptical scrutiny. A closeup look had been all that was needed to cinch Hooky's suspicions. Stark hoped the barkeep woke up with a nasty headache.

"Everybody sit back down," he ordered aloud. "This

shotgun's a repeater, not a double-barrel. After two loads, I'm just getting started.''

Gun hands were twitching, but the hardcases slowly resumed their seats. Amid the rustle of clothing, Stark caught the near-simultaneous clicks of two pistols coming to full cock.

''Hold it, Zeke,'' a cultured voice said coolly. ''Bad idea. Let the hammer down nice and easy.'' As he spoke, one of the lawyers rose smoothly to his feet. He held a revolver leveled competently at a disreputable-looking hombre occupying a nearby table.

Zeke twisted a stubbled face around to eye his challenger. What he saw in the lawyer's steady gaze made him obey his orders and reluctantly holster his gun.

''Good man.''

The lawyer moved clear of his chair and stepped deftly through the clutter of tables. His colleagues observed him with bemused expressions. He was younger than Stark, with a tall, rugged build that his suit and vest couldn't conceal. Some women might figure him as handsome. He handled his gun as if he'd used it before.

Once free of the tables, he faced the roomful of men with the same ease he might've displayed in a courtroom. He was careful to stay within Stark's range of vision.

''Mr. Stark here is giving you fellows good advice,'' he announced to his captive audience. ''Just sit tight and let him ease out of here peaceful-like, so nobody gets hurt. That bounty isn't worth anybody's life.'' He cut a sideward glance at Stark. ''I'll cover you.''

Stark tried to watch the whole room at once, including

this gun-toting lawyer. ''Some folks would say you're backing a losing hand,'' he suggested dryly.

''I'm not partial to lynchings, and that's close to what this is. Kincaid's not in charge of making the laws around here. Besides, I've got a vested interest, you might say. Name's James Mathers. I'm the local prosecutor. I know most of these men, one way or another, and I'd hate to see any of them get shot up. I figure I'm saving myself and the judge some work as well. And I don't want the job of sorting out jurisdiction in the middle of the river.''

''Obliged,'' Stark said. ''I can take it from here.''

''I'll stick with you for now,'' Mathers answered. He jerked his head toward the door. ''Go on. I'll watch your back.''

Stark edged toward the door. He was careful not to turn away from Mathers. An attorney could collect the reward as well as the next man, even an attorney who professed good faith. But Mathers was as good as his word. He paced Stark, keeping the watching men under his gun.

Holding the shotgun one-handed, finger taut on the trigger, Stark reached to open the door. He risked a quick glance over his shoulder. In the illumination from the saloon, he could see that the deck outside was clear. The rush of fresh air felt good in his nostrils. It smelled of safety.

''I'm keeping this door covered,'' he promised grimly. ''Anybody other than the shyster sticks his head out, I'll blow it right back in.''

As he sidestepped through the door he caught a glimpse of the shaggy wolfer where he still leaned against the far wall. The man hadn't so much as moved during the face-off, but his eyes were no longer blank, and his stare was no longer dull. He watched Stark with the same raptness that he might watch a renegade lobo that had evaded his traps. Stark carried that image with him into the night.

He stopped before he stepped onto the plank bridge. Mathers followed him out, covering his back as he'd promised.

Stark motioned with his shotgun. ''You first.'' Friend or foe, he wanted the lawyer ahead of him on the walkway.

''Trusting soul, aren't you?'' Mathers said lightly and complied with the command. He moved quickly over the unsteady boards.

Crab walking, Stark followed in his wake. He kept the shotgun leveled at the boxy structure of the Ark. He alternated glances at it with quick looks toward the far shore past the gliding shape of Mathers. It was full night now. The moon cast sharp silver ricochets off the swift waters of the river. A misstep, and he'd be swept away. The river might collect the bounty. The bridge sagged even further as the distance widened between them and the saloon.

''Could be trouble ahead,'' Mathers informed him tersely.

Stark looked and saw he was right. A handful of riders had pounded up to the hitching rail, no doubt cowhands or rowdies intent on a good time. They were already swinging from their mounts amid raucous laughter and yells.

From the Ark, another voice sounded. Stark swung

his attention back there and saw the burly figure of Hooky lurch into view through the doorway, hook waving high overhead. The silhouetted figures of other enraged customers milled behind him.

"That's the Peacemaker on the bridge!" Hooky's shout carried clearly across the water. "There's five thousand for the man who brings him down! Don't let him get past you fellows!"

Gunfire rang out as one of Hooky's cronies threw lead. The newcomers on the shore were already reacting to the news. Plainly, they were no strangers to knowledge of the reward. In moments, Stark reckoned, he and his ally would be caught in a withering cross fire.

"Get down!" he snapped.

Mathers didn't hesitate. He dropped to one knee, ducking his head low. Stark didn't hesitate either. Flinging the shotgun to his shoulder, he fired, levered, and fired again. The ten-gauge blasts rolled across the water like cannon reports. In rapid succession a load of buckshot, then a solid slug pounded the wooden wall of the Ark.

Stark had aimed high, but the buckshot spread like a swarm of hornets coming out of a prodded hive. There were screams and hollers. The bar patrons dropped flat or dived back inside. At least one tumbled off the dock with a resounding splash. Light shone suddenly from the hole the solid slug had punched all the way through the massive boards of the wall.

Before the commotion could settle, Stark wheeled smoothly and gave the rounders on the shore the same treatment: a meal of buckshot with a slug for dessert. Men and horses scattered. A couple made it into their saddles. The rest took to their heels as their mounts stampeded in all directions.

"Make for shore!" Stark barked. He dropped his right hand to the butt of his Colt, but no return fire seemed forthcoming.

Mathers legged it hard toward the riverbank, his boots clattering on the planks, his arms spread a little for balance. Stark was close on his heels, reloading the shotgun by touch as he moved. He looked over his shoulder at every other step, but no more gunfire winked at them from the Ark. Hooky and his customers were keeping their heads down.

In moments, Mathers stepped off the bridge onto the shore. He holstered his gun as Stark joined him. The lawyer was panting a bit.

Stark's breath was coming a little faster than usual too. "I'm beholden to you," he said, then added, "For a lawyer, you're pretty handy with that six-gun."

Mathers shrugged. "Sometimes it's the only way to get a verdict."

"Or an acquittal," Stark said.

Mathers chuckled, then sobered. "Is what that fellow said true? Did you kill Kincaid's son?"

Stark nodded. "He was a stage robber. I was on the trail of him and his pards when they bushwhacked me. No choice. It was them or me. They called the play." It was rare, he reflected, that he felt the need to justify himself to any man.

Mathers was nodding thoughtfully. "I suspected something of the sort. I expected nothing less of you. Prudence—Miss McKay—has spoken highly of you indeed."

Stark looked at him sharply.

Mathers gave a chuckle that seemed suddenly a little strained. "Oh, not to worry. I've encountered Miss McKay in court at one time or another. I've even served as cocounsel with her. She is a most able barrister. Our acquaintance is strictly professional, I assure you. She did happen to mention that she had represented you on one occasion. You're really a most fortunate fellow." Something made him break off abruptly.

"Never mind all that," Stark growled, wondering why the deuce the shyster was rambling in such a fashion. And what had he meant by that last crack?

"I need you to get word to Marshal Nix in Guthrie," Stark went on. It figured that he was running short on time in Purcell, now that his presence was known.

"My pleasure," Mathers said quickly.

"Tell Nix that I've found out who's responsible for the bounty. Tell him it's Lucius Kincaid, and that I'm going after him. I've got a bounty of my own to collect. It's Kincaid's life. I'll be back when I've collected it."

Mathers was staring at him in the gloom. He drew away a little. "I'll see that Nix gets the message," he promised hoarsely.

Stark hesitated. "You going to be safe here?" he queried.

Mathers gave quick reassurance. "I'll be fine."

Stark took him at his word. He turned to his horse. Voices were sounding and lights were showing up in the town proper, no doubt in response to the gunfire.

He kept his shotgun in hand as he reined his horse, Red, sharply about and sent him along the slippery riverbank at a gallop.

"Good luck!" Mathers shouted after him.

Chapter Four

Stark rode by day as he pushed deeper into the largely uninhabited realms of the Indian Lands. The darkness of night provided cover for a hunted man, but it also provided cover for his hunters. Daylight travel was swifter, and allowed him to check his back trail as well as giving him a chance to see what lay ahead.

The terrain consisted of rolling grassland scarred by the occasional wooded courses of meandering creeks. He avoided skylining himself, and where a waterway matched his route, he stayed to the cover of the fringing underbrush and towering cottonwoods. Wisps of the cottony seeds were beginning to dance on the breeze like huge out-of-season snowflakes. They tickled his nose when a gust sent them flitting past.

He was an old hand at traveling this way, but it was usually when he was doing the hunting, not when he was the one being hunted. Still, he reminded himself, things had changed after the Ark. Now that he had the name of Lucius Kincaid, he was doing some hunting of his own.

He knew generally where Kincaid's holdings lay. He had heard something of the man, and the illicit empire of land he held by right of possession. Initially, he was said to have leased a huge expanse of grasslands from the Tribes. Such arrangements weren't uncommon. Ranchers did it for pasture, and some outlaw gangs had been known to do so in order to ensure the presence of a hideout.

But once in possession, and having erected what amounted to a fortress to protect himself, Kincaid had called in a small army of gunmen to side him, and simply reneged on his deal with the Indians. No tribe in their right mind would seek to oust a white man by force, not even one who had cheated them. Intervention by the U.S. government would be swift and certain.

So Kincaid was left to rule his kingdom far back in the Indian territory. The source of his wealth, as well as his life before coming to the territories, remained a mystery. Not many folks doubted, however, that he had the money to make good on the bounty.

Until he'd heard it in the Ark, Stark had made no connection between the hapless young stage robber, who'd tried his hand at bushwhacking the wrong man, and the mysterious prairie despot. He hadn't even known the kid's name until Nix had told him back at the beginning of this affair. He'd never heard of the senior Kincaid having a child, much less a would-be hellion and outlaw.

Stark shook his head regretfully as he recalled the sudden flurry of violence that had tallied three more men dead under his guns.

The ambush had been clumsy, but he'd still ridden into it, not expecting such resistance from greenhorn outlaws. When they'd opened up from the shelter of a thicket, he had returned fire with the shotgun, emptying it, and virtually shredding the bushes in the process.

Bunched together behind the flimsy cover, none of them had survived the fusillade. It had been over almost before Stark realized it had begun. His reactions had all been born of reflex and experience, but they'd saved his life and cost Marty Kincaid and his compadres theirs.

The three of them paid dearly for their inexperience, and now he was once again having to rely on his reflexes to survive.

Stark felt his teeth grind together. *Don't count the money out yet, Kincaid,* he thought darkly as he pulled Red to a halt.

He had ridden almost to the crest of a high ridge, and he dismounted with his powerful field glasses in hand. Crouching at first, then dropping at last to his belly, he worked his way to the top of the ridge. Parting the grass, careful to keep the glasses shielded beneath the brim of his Stetson, he began a deliberate survey of his back trail across an entire half-span of the compass.

Nothing alarmed him. He saw the fleet shapes of a handful of the wild horses that still haunted these remote reaches of the prairie. There was a dun stallion and his small harem of mares. A colt frolicked in the tall grass.

Stark kept his glasses on them for a few moments. He was pleased by the sight of them, but saddened by what he knew lay ahead for them and their kind. Mustangers would eventually run them to ground, or cattlemen would kill them to clear good pastureland. They were free, but they were living on borrowed time.

Unexpectedly, the stallion's head jerked up. His ears pricked forward alertly as he stared hard in the direction Stark had been traveling. Hastily, Stark squirmed about to aim his lenses in that direction, twirling the knob to bring the countryside into focus. Mentally, he upbraided himself. He'd let his attention be distracted too long by the wild horses.

A pair of riders was topping a hill. They were headed in his direction. Their appearance had spooked the wild stallion and his mares. Stark swept the rest of the horizon, then settled the field glasses on the pair.

He had noticed more horsemen on the move than was usual in these parts, he reflected. He'd brushed aside the notion that Kincaid's bounty might've set a good percentage of the outlaws and drifters holed up in the Lands on the prowl for him, sparked by the news that he could be heading for Kincaid's stronghold. Now he was wondering if that notion might not be right. A powerful lot of men in these parts bore real or imagined grudges against him. Open season on the Peacemaker might've stirred even the meekest to join the hunt.

Eyeing this latest pair, he had no doubts as to their intentions. Well armed, they had the hard look of adventurers or renegades. Their matching black dusters and flat-crowned hats made them appear like a mirror-image mirage created by the glaring overhead sun. As they rode, they kept their heads turning, constantly scanning the grasslands. One of them saw the wild horses and pointed. Sharp eyes. They didn't deviate from their course.

Whoever these hombres were, they were bad news. Stark eased himself back down the slope. He returned the glasses to his saddlebag as he mounted. Red tossed his head, sensing the tension in his rider, perhaps scenting the approaching horses on the vagrant breeze.

Using the ridge for cover, Stark moved out. If he

continued in the direction he was bound, he would run head-on into the pair of long riders. Instead, he swung out so as to circle clear of them. It irked him to do so, but there was no need in confronting them, whatever their intentions, if he could avoid it.

Keeping the rolling terrain between him and the pair, he traveled to the south in a wide arc that would eventually bring him back to the northeasterly direction he coveted. He kept Red to an easy lope that covered the ground, but wasn't likely to betray his presence by the vibrations of the sorrel's drumming hooves.

He had covered several miles, and was beginning to swing back north, when he halted to let Red blow. Dismounting, he again snaked to the summit of a hillock and used the field glasses to survey the countryside. As he looked, he felt his entire body go taut. The long riders were angling toward him at a steady lope. The rolling terrain he had tried to use to conceal himself had also served to block his view of them. They were closer to him than when he'd first seen them, as though they had cut across the arc he had made rather than simply following his trail.

His planning and the long extra miles had been for nought. Somehow they'd spotted him or cut his trail. More likely the former, he thought, remembering the sharp-eyed one pointing out the wild horses to his pard.

But whatever had happened, he was certain they were after him. He scowled darkly. He didn't hanker to tangle with these hombres. They looked to know their business. Besides, he'd had a gutful of killing since this mess began.

He'd told Prudence that he chose his wars, and that

he fought only for causes he considered just. But he'd been forced into this war with Kincaid, albeit for a just cause. The long riders were little better than outlaws; they didn't have any legitimate business in trying to collect an illegal bounty. In a larger sense, though, they were nothing but Kincaid's tools—hired guns, bearing some kinship, however remote, with himself. Knocking down hired guns wasn't going to win this war; it would just add to his own grim tally. And there'd always be more of them so long as the bounty was offered.

Stark bared his teeth in a bitter snarl. Yeah, he'd fight this formidable pair if he had to. But killing them—even given that he could—wasn't the answer. Far better to stay out of their way, and save the killing for the man who'd turned them into his dupes in the first place.

He calculated rapidly. So far they'd managed to anticipate his moves and maybe catch an occasional glimpse of him. Thereby, they'd closed the gap between them to a considerable extent. They couldn't know for sure who he was, which meant they might be a little reluctant to try to down him with rifle work. But he couldn't set too much store by their merciful natures. Any man on a big sorrel was likely fair game.

He could play tag with them the rest of the day and let them slowly herd him farther and farther from his course. He was in no mood to let himself get so far sidetracked. Making up the lost ground would only increase the risk of encountering more bounty-hungry stalkers.

He glanced gaugingly at Red. The sorrel was as fine a horse as he'd ever forked. This present stop had been as much for his own benefit as for the stallion's. Several days of steady travel had only served to tone and condition the sorrel's sleek muscles and bring his coordination to a fine edge. If they could get out of rifle range, he'd be willing to bet high stakes on Red against any horse on the range in a straight cross-country run.

And he'd be betting pretty high stakes this time.

Using the field glasses, he laid out a map in his head of a route over the grassy hills and ridges that might put him out of reach of the pair's saddle guns before he came into the open. He checked their location one last time, estimating time and speed. Moving swiftly then, he returned to the sorrel and ran gentle hands over the animal's body, murmuring softly the whole time. Red's sleek muscles trembled eagerly beneath his touch.

Satisfied that nothing was amiss, Stark swung astride. He eased the stallion into a gallop, using the irregular lay of the land to shelter him as he pulled away from his unsuspecting pursuers. To them, he was cash on the hoof, he mused wryly.

At length he emerged from a draw with flat, open grassland stretching away from him. He laid the reins light against Red's flexing neck, turning his course gradually once more to the northwest. Red's easy gallop never faltered.

Stark looked back, his body balancing with the roll of the saddle. The long riders were beyond easy rifle range, but still he saw a white puff of smoke roll up from one of them. The faint crack of the shot came a moment later. Stark ducked automatically, but wherever it went, the bullet came nowhere close. So much for banking on their reluctance to gun down a stranger.

He could imagine them putting spurs to their mounts.

He'd given them a little bit of an advantage by running at a wide angle to their course, but even when they cut the angle, they'd still be far enough off that luck would be more to credit than skill if they managed to nail him with their saddle guns.

They must've figured the same, for after that first fruitless shot, they concentrated on riding. And, recognizing the caliber of his mount, they were too good as horsemen to gamble everything on an all-out sprint at this point.

The wind rushed past Stark's face as Red carried him on. He eased the sorrel's speed up a notch to a run. Red was covering ground now, although he was good for yet more speed when the time came. Stark prayed no prairie-dog holes or other unseen obstacles that could trip up a running horse lay in their path.

On they streaked across the prairie. His pursuers had cut off the angle and rode directly in his wake. They'd gained only a bit in falling in behind him. For now they seemed content to stay hard on his tail, pushing him a little, but unwilling to risk breaking their horses' wind until his own had tired.

And they seemed to have good horses, which boded a long chase, with no guarantees of the outcome. It might yet come down to bullets and powder smoke between them.

Stark felt the powerful rhythmic surge of the animal beneath him. So far, Red was enjoying the opportunity to run. He was showing no signs of strain. Stark felt a twinge of regret at what he was fixing to ask of him.

The grass seemed to flow beneath Red's flashing hooves. High overhead, Stark glimpsed the wide-winged silhouette of a drifting hawk. What would this chase across the vast plain look like to the circling predator?

Red's breathing grew heavier. Stark let his body move with the surge and flow of the horse, lessening the burden of his weight. He twisted his head about to peer back and saw that the long riders had managed to narrow the gap. They were beginning to push their mounts.

Another quarter-mile and he looked back again. The pursuers had drawn yet a bit closer. Both of them had their horses running flat-out. Stark could see the jerking motions of their arms as they used their reins for quirts to urge their animals on. They'd be plying their spurs cruelly too. At last, they were gambling they could run him to ground before their horses played out.

He was gambling they couldn't. He leaned far forward over Red's neck and reached out a palm to touch the sweat-soaked coat. "Go, Red," he said tightly, and drummed his own spurless heels against the sorrel's ribs.

Red's stride lengthened. He stretched out until he seemed to fly across the grassland, hooves barely touching the ground. His shadow raced beside him. Stark felt the increased wind of their passage pluck at his hat and his clothing. A fierce exhilaration pumped in his blood.

Flecks of foam began to form around Red's mouth. Sweat turned his red coat to black. Still he ran, speed never faltering. Stark imagined the proud heart pounding within the wide chest. He could feel the unceasing flex and roll and play of the muscles powered by that heart. Briefly, it seemed it was his own heart that drove the stallion, so close were they to being one.

He didn't know how many miles they had covered since this death race had started. Ahead loomed the vague shapes of hills which had not even been on the horizon when they'd begun. He threw a look back. The long riders' horses were keeping up with Red's head-long pace.

"Go, boy!" Stark called to Red's laid-back ears. "Go!"

Red went. Incredibly, his stride increased once more, and Stark's breath caught in his throat with amazement and fear. No animal could maintain this speed for long, not even Red. It would kill him as surely as a bullet from one of the bounty hunters' guns. Before another mile was past, Stark knew he'd have to pull up and take his chances against their rifles.

The barrel of Red's body was heaving with every straining breath. Stark twisted his head around, blinking the wind tears from his eyes. For a moment he couldn't be sure, then a grin pulled his lips away from his teeth. The gap had widened; he was certain of it. The figures of the long riders were a tiny bit smaller. Red was pulling steadily ahead of them. Stark's whoop was torn away by the wind.

It didn't mean the chase was over. Red could still falter; the bounty hunters' horses might still have enough left to overtake them if he did.

He'd give them something to think about, Stark decided. He drew the Colt Peacemaker and stretched his arm back toward them. Working hammer and trigger, he emptied it in a barrage of rolling thunder that was left quickly behind. It was mostly for show. The chances of scoring a hit at this range from the back of a running

horse were practically nil. But they would see the gun-
smoke, know he was shooting at them, know he still
had plenty of fight left if they did catch up.

Maybe one of the bullets came close. Maybe one of
the pair flinched. Or maybe the grueling race at last took
its toll. One man's horse faltered, missing stride. Its
head bowed and it lurched drunkenly against its companion. Men and horses went down in a flurry of hooves
and tails and waving arms.

Stark felt himself sag in the saddle. Even if they got
their horses up uninjured, there was no way they could
continue the chase. Red had run the other animals into
the ground.

"Enough, fellow," Stark's voice choked. He let the
sorrel feel just the gentlest tug on the reins. "Easy now.
You've done it. Good boy."

Gradually Red's gait slackened. He dropped from a
run to a gallop, to a lope, then at last into a staggering
walk. Stark halted him and dismounted as softly as he
could. Every muscle beneath the sweat-soaked hide was
trembling. Stark was trembling some himself. He unsheathed his field glasses and lifted them to his eyes.

Both men and horses were back on their feet, looking
tired and shaken, even at this distance. The men were
staring in his direction. They were making no effort to
continue the chase or start throwing lead. Stark watched
them for a moment. One of them wearily raised something to his eyes, and Stark caught the glint of reflected
sunlight. He realized the fellow was returning his scrutiny with glasses of his own.

After a span of seconds the watcher gave a tired wave
of acknowledgment. Stark almost smiled. A warrior's

salute. The long riders had been trying to kill him for an unholy cause, but they'd been worthy enough foes for all that.

Stark raised his hand and sketched a salute in return.

He turned once more to Red. The sorrel's breathing had slowed some. The wooded hills weren't far away. Trees indicated water and shade. Stark caught the reins and led the winded horse in that direction at a walk. He'd let Red—and himself—rest for a spell once they had reached the shelter of the hills.

Then they'd have to move on.

Chapter Five

Bold as brass, the man they called Gundance rode up to the towering stone edifice rising out of the prairie. He'd heard it described as a castle and as a fortress, and he figured it was something of a crossbreed of the two. Reluctantly, he had to admit to himself that he was impressed. It had taken a heap of work—and *dinero*—to lift this structure up out of the sparse native stone of the area.

He took it all in as he approached. Dark stone, three stories, leaded glass in some of the windows, even a sort of lookout tower perched atop it. He could see the figure of a man with a rifle up there silhouetted by the late-afternoon sun.

A couple more men were waiting for him on the railroad-tie porch that stretched the width of the house. Two-for-a-dollar gunhands, he mused with a mental sneer. He'd bypassed or talked his way through the ranks of them that were patrolling the surrounding grassland for miles around. Their numbers alone must've cost a pretty penny.

This pair looked to be a cut above the average. Side by side, hands on their hips near their gun butts, they confronted him from the shade of the veranda as he pulled to a halt. The steel-dust gelding, responsive to his

49

every whim now, stood like a graven image. No more going loco over a few gunshots.

He used the forefinger of his left hand to poke back the brim of his Stetson. His right hand was close to his gun butt too.

He waited until the taller of the pair lost patience and started to speak; then he cut him off in a drawl: "This wouldn't happen to be the Kincaid homestead, now would it? Reckon it must be. Either that or a great big stone bawdyhouse. You boys the bouncers? Keep the riffraff out?"

They didn't like that; he hadn't meant for them to. The taller one cocked his head. "Yeah, we keep the riffraff out," he growled. "Who's asking?"

"My mother called me Lance. You fellows can do the same."

The eyes of the tall one widened, then grew narrow in speculation.

"You still ain't answered my question," Trowbridge prodded deliberately. "This where the high and mighty Lucius Kincaid hangs his hat?"

"This is the Kincaid place," the tall one said carefully.

His companion bridled, then squared his shoulders belligerently. "State your business, then hit the trail, pard."

Trowbridge heard the familiar eager humming of his own nerves. "I don't know you well enough to be your pard," he said coolly, then added contemptuously, *"Pard."*

The short one stiffened. His taller companion inclined

his head and said in a whisper that reached Trowbridge clearly, "It's Gundance."

Some starch went out of the short hombre. The humming faded from Trowbridge's nerves. He sensed its departure with disappointment. There'd be no dancing with this one, unless he prodded a lot harder. Riling him had been a fool's move anyway, but sometimes a man's hankerings just got in the way of common sense.

"You're him? You're Gundance?" the short one pressed.

"I told you; it's Lance to my pards."

"You here about the bounty?"

This one was going to back down, right enough, but he wanted to save a little face in doing it. "I'm here about *a* bounty," Trowbridge conceded.

"You think you can take him? You think you can beat the Peacemaker?" The little gunslinger's eyes glittered.

"I expect I could. That is, if I had reason enough to."

"The boss will pay you five thousand dollars if you kill Stark. That's plenty of reason!"

"No," Gundance corrected softly. "That's what he'll pay *you* if you kill him."

Puzzlement and a reborn truculence etched the smaller man's face. "I've always wondered," he said slowly, "just how many men it is you've killed."

The humming came back nice and clear. Trowbridge cocked his head a little so he could hear it better. "Ain't rightly kept track," he lied. "But I'll tell you this."

"I'm listening."

"There's three kinds of men that I kill: ones I'm hunt-

ing; ones that try to kill me; and the third type, ones
that I just plain want to kill.''

The tall one inclined his head toward his compadre
again. ''Go tell Mr. Kincaid he's here,'' he ordered. His
eyes never left Trowbridge's smiling face.

For a moment the smaller man hesitated. Then he
looked into Trowbridge's wide eyes and wilted all over
again. Swallowing hard, he turned and stomped across
the porch. He disappeared through the massive oak
doors.

Trowbridge regarded the tall gunslinger curiously.

The latter shrugged. ''No point in seeing a good man
killed,'' he said tonelessly.

''Plenty of point,'' Trowbridge said, but he didn't
press the issue. This one had sand, and he wasn't stupid
enough to pick a fight he couldn't win.

They waited in an almost companionable silence until
the little one reappeared. ''Mr. Kincaid wants to see
you,'' he reported sullenly.

''Well, now, fancy that, would you?'' Trowbridge
gave them both an easygoing grin, turned the steel-dust
until it was between him and the pair, and stepped from
the saddle. ''Obliged for your help, gentlemen,'' he said
as he mounted the steps and went past them.

Just inside the door was a big, powerfully built man
in a suit that looked all wrong on him. A pair of leggings
and a bare-knuckle ring would've been more suited to
him than the high paneled foyer with its towering mir-
rored hall trees and European grandfather clock.

His mauled face split in a grin that was every bit as
arrogant as Trowbridge's own. He didn't look to be
packing iron. ''I'm Break. The boss is waiting.''

"Well, so am I. Let's get this outfit moving."

He followed the broad, rolling shoulders past a parlor and a library. A woman was just emerging from the roomful of bookshelves. She almost bumped into Trowbridge, then recovered but didn't move back very far.

"Hello," she said throatily.

Trowbridge smiled widely. "Hello," he echoed.

Studying her, he thought she looked as out of place for a library as the butler had for the entryway. Maybe he hadn't been far off the money in calling Kincaid's homestead a bawdyhouse. A tight dress, too much makeup, and lazy, knowing eyes told her tale.

"You must be Mrs. Kincaid," he said brightly.

"Yeah, that's right," she answered with a dryness that showed her appreciation of his sly wit. "I'm Nona."

"And I'm Lance, Miss Nona." Trowbridge decided he liked her.

"The boss is waiting on you," the butler rumbled. He had turned back to scowl disapprovingly.

Nona lifted one of her small fists to her scarlet lips and kissed her own knuckle. Her nails were as red as her lips. A neat lipstick print was left on her knuckle. "You better go with Break, Lance," she suggested. "Maybe I'll see you again before you leave."

"And maybe I'll see you."

She gave him a lazy, provocative smile and slipped past him.

"Mr. Kincaid's sister?" he queried to Break's back as the prizefighter led him down the wide hallway.

Break didn't answer.

With little formality he ushered the manhunter into a

study heavy with the layered scents of upholstered leather, whiskey, and fine cigars. Trowbridge breathed in with satisfaction. Navajo rugs were underfoot. The mounted heads of buffalo and longhorn cattle regarded him glassily from the walls. He noted one old mossy-back with a horn span of a good seven feet. This, he thought, looked about like what an Eastern millionaire would figure a cattle baron's den should look like. So far as he knew, Kincaid didn't have a steer to his name.

The millionaire himself was in one of several uphol-stered chairs, puffing a thick cigar into life. And he wasn't alone. The blond woman who had bent down close to light the cigar was just straightening up. She blew out the match with a pursing of her lips that was almost identical to the kiss Nona had bestowed on her own knuckle. Aside from the color of their hair, the two women could've come from the same litter.

Another sister? Another wife? Trowbridge wondered wryly. Kincaid had imported all the luxuries here to his homestead.

"Thanks, hon. We've got company. Bring us a little something from the bar," her master instructed.

She swayed obediently toward a gleaming mahogany bar that would've graced the finest of saloons. Kincaid heaved himself up out of the massive chair which had supported his bulk.

"Lucius Kincaid, at your service." He extended a soft hand aglitter with diamond rings. Trowbridge couldn't feel any bones beneath the flesh.

The millionaire was a great porker of a man with a little pointed beard and carefully trimmed mustache. His features seemed lost in the fleshiness of his face. He wore trousers and a flaring scarlet silk robe embroidered with entwining golden dragons. Slippers of the same fabric encased his feet. If he hadn't seen just how much power this man could wield from his remote stronghold, Trowbridge would've laughed out loud at the sight of him.

Instead, he accepted the offer of a seat, a glass of sipping whiskey, one of the premium cigars, and a repeat of the same intimate lighting ceremony he'd seen the blond perform for Kincaid. Her owner didn't look to be offended. He seemed to enjoy her performance even when he wasn't the recipient. Finished, the blond faded into the background. Break, the bodyguard, had positioned himself by the door. Trowbridge was careful to keep him in the edge of his vision.

Glass in one hand, cigar in the other, Kincaid sipped, then puffed with sensual satisfaction before leaning back in his chair. His dark eyes were buried so deep in the folds of his face that they were hard to read.

Trowbridge tasted his own whiskey, smacked his lips, then set the glass carefully aside. It was quality stuff, but a man who lived by his gun couldn't afford to be much of a drinker; not if he wanted to keep on living. Alcohol slowed a man's wits and his gun hand.

He kept the cigar in his left hand, wanting his right free. For all his physical softness, Kincaid struck him as a mighty dangerous man. Black leather gleamed briefly within one voluminous sleeve of the scarlet robe, and Trowbridge recognized the same kind of hideout rig some gamblers favored, the sort that could pop a little derringer almost instantly into Kincaid's pudgy hand. The millionaire might not need Break as a bodyguard.

"I understand you have some business to discuss with me, Mr. Trowbridge. Or do you prefer Gundance?"

Trowbridge could imagine this man in a business suit dominating a New York or Chicago boardroom. "We might have business we can do," he confirmed aloud, deliberately ignoring Kincaid's inquiry. "That's why I came to see you."

Kincaid's smile was no more than a crease in his face. "Well, I'm pleased to make your acquaintance. Even back East there are tales and rumors of your exploits as a hunter of men."

"Just the reason I'm here. I understand you're willing to pay a great deal of money to have a man killed."

"One man in particular. James Stark. The Peace-maker." Dark flames seemed to glitter from the slits that were his eyes.

"And I have to wonder why you'd invest your money in a thing like that?"

Kincaid sipped and puffed. The flames faded into faint gleams. "I came out here some years back to devote myself to the life of seclusion and leisure to which my business successes have entitled me. Fine food, liquor, cigars. Companionship." He twitched his cigar vaguely in the direction of the blond.

None of which explained a stone fortress and an army of hired guns, Trowbridge reflected. He drew at his own cigar and kept silent. Smoke hung in a haze between them.

"To my surprise, I discovered that I had left behind me a son. The result of, shall we say, a pleasurable dalliance. Learning that the boy's mother had succumbed to a distasteful illness, I made arrangements to have him come live here with me. When something is mine, I do not like to leave it in the possession of others. Nor do I like to have it taken away from me.''

''And that's what Stark did?''

Kincaid's nod created new chins. ''Exactly. He killed my son.''

''Make any difference that your son was an outlaw, and that he and his pards tried to kill Stark from ambush?''

''Not a whit. Marty chose to run with the wild dogs. I did the same thing in my youth, although in a far different environment. Marty's death by Stark's hand is what counts with me, regardless of the circumstances. Frankly, however, I'm a little surprised to have you arrive here expressing an interest in this matter. From what I understand, you interceded to save Stark's life in Guthrie when an attempt was made to earn the reward on his head.''

Trowbridge showed him a slow smile. ''That's simple enough to understand. I didn't want anybody else collecting bounty money on the Peacemaker. That privilege is reserved for me.''

''So you are interested in killing him,'' Kincaid asserted with vicious eagerness.

''Oh, I'm interested in trying my hand at bringing him down,'' Trowbridge affirmed lazily. ''But not for any paltry five thousand dollars.''

''What? What's that?''

Trowbridge leaned forward, elbows on his knees. He spoke intently. ''You're willing to pay five thousand dollars to any two-bit hardcase or *pistolero* who can bring down James Stark. Well, I'm here to tell you it won't happen, unless one of them gets awful lucky. Stark didn't need my help in Guthrie, not against the saloon sweepings your bounty sicced on him. The Peacemaker will eat their kind alive and come away hungry."

"But you can take him. Is that what you're telling me?" Kincaid was just as intent. His whiskey and cigar seemed forgotten.

"If I can't, nobody can. Look at it this way. I'm the best there is at what I do, and if you want the best, you pay a premium for it, just like with your whiskey and your cigars. Besides, as good as I am, I calculate the Peacemaker might be the one man alive who would have an outside chance at beating me. If I'm going up against him, I want to be paid what my services are worth."

"And that is?"

"Ten thousand dollars," Trowbridge said flatly.

Kincaid tasted of each of his vices again. "You interest me, Gundance. But are you as good as they, and you, say? What are your credentials?"

"All of my references are dead," Trowbridge said dryly.

"And how many would that be?"

"I've lost track," Trowbridge lied as he had earlier.

In truth, he remembered each of them clearly, remembered each time how the seductive humming of his nerves had seemed to rise to a crescendo in his ears when the moment of truth arrived. But the numbers, like the humming, were his own business.

"Hey," he said aloud, "do you want a head count, or do you want James Stark dead?"

Kincaid regarded him from those shrewd slits of eyes. "Ten thousand dollars if you're the one who brings him down. Somebody else downs him, even with your help, and you get nothing."

"I don't need help," Trowbridge said. "And if I fail, I won't be around to argue with you about partial payment."

"Fair enough."

Trowbridge took a final pull on the cigar, then stubbed it out. "Okay," he said decisively. "I'll want a room on the top floor with a window looking out front. I'll also want access at a moment's notice to areas that provide a view of the rear of the house. And I'll need the run of the place. I won't interefere with your men, or give them orders, but they're not to get in my way."

Bafflement stretched Kincaid's fleshy features. "What are you talking about?" he demanded. "Aren't you going after him?"

Trowbridge smiled happily. "I won't have to. I'll just sit back and wait for him to come here."

"Exactly what is that supposed to mean?"

"The Peacemaker's on his way here," Trowbridge declared with certainty. "By now, he's discovered you're the one who posted the bounty, and he's coming after you. Your cordon of outriders, your hired guns, and those two tinhorns on the front porch won't stop him. Neither will your stumblebum prizefighter." He jerked his head toward Break.

Kincaid had regained his aplomb. He sniffed disdainfully. "I wouldn't discount my men. I've spent good money to hire the best." He ignored Trowbridge's own disdainful sniff. "And I wouldn't discount Break. He killed a man with his fists in a barroom brawl back East. I saw it happen. It cost him his title. I hired him. He's fast. Put him in the same room as a man with a gun, and he'll lay him out with his fists before the gun can come into play. I've seen that happen too.''

Trowbridge let his sardonic grin answer for him. "So, do we still have a deal?'' he asked with a lift of his lip.

"Do you guarantee you'll deliver Stark to me?''

"I'll do better than that. I'll make him dance for you.''

Chapter Six

Stark built a smokeless fire and kept it alive only long enough to brew coffee and fix beans and bacon. During the day he'd gotten by mostly from chewing on jerky as he rode. His camp was far back in a wide strip of woodland along the path of a deep creek bed. After allowing Red to drink, he'd filled his canteen, then moved well away from the water before settling down.

Red had fully recovered from the cross-country race with the long riders a couple of days before. Earlier, Stark had spotted a lone cowpoke. After first observing him carefully with his field glasses, he'd stopped the fellow and gotten directions to the Kincaid stronghold. The cowpoke knew of it and advised Stark that he'd been warned off the range a few days back by heavily armed riders. He seemed ignorant of the bounty. Stark thanked him but kept an eye on him until he'd disappeared. Learning that Kincaid had his gunsels on the prowl didn't surprise him. If the millionaire didn't know he was coming, he at least suspected it.

With Red nearby, he brooded now over his coffee. Night always claimed the woods early. The tops of the trees seemed to reach up to catch the darkness and claw it down to the spidery grasp of the branches below. A raccoon gave its eerie trill, and a possum snorted and snuffled like a miniature hog in the blanket of old leaves on the damp forest floor. A nighthawk flew silently past like a lonely seeking spirit.

An image of Prudence flickered into Stark's mind from somewhere. Funny—with his mental eyes he usually pictured her in one of her light moods, vibrant and smiling, rather than angry with him or his ways, as so often seemed to be the case in reality. She had once hidden out with him on a night like this, while ruthless men hunted them both. She'd shown her mettle then. He regretted not having been on better terms with her when he'd left Guthrie on this quest.

He was almost dozing, he realized, and roused himself to make one last circuit of the area. Overhead, through the spring foliage, he caught glimpses of a night sky so bright with stars that it almost hurt his eyes. A man would be able to see a long ways out on the open expanse of the prairie, he calculated.

Coyotes had begun to yip back and forth when he returned to his camp and spread out his bedroll. Tiredness weighed down on him as if he was a toting a heavy saddle, but the hair-trigger sharpness of his nerves resisted sleep for a spell. Red made a pretty fair watchdog, but he still had his Colt by his hand when he drifted off.

His fingers closed on it automatically as he awakened. He lay still. Something had stirred him, set the blood pumping with warning through his veins. He probed the night with his ears and nostrils. What had alerted him?

Nearby, Red snorted, and a horse whinnied in reply from deeper in the woods. Stark was out of the bedroll and to the sorrel's side in a trice. He pressed his palm to the animal's velvety muzzle to forestall further sound, and waited tensely. He had to slow his own breathing some in order to hear.

"What's got into that nag?" a man's muffled voice demanded.

"Don't know. Maybe he smelled another horse," a second rough voice replied.

"Naw, another horse would've answered. Probably a coyote or some such critter spooked it. Put it with them other nags."

The sorrel's training had kept him from reacting to the presence of the other horses. Could be, that had saved his own hide, Stark reflected. It sounded as though there were more than two men out there. Who were they? What disreputable business brought them here?

Whoever they were, he'd be better off avoiding them, he decided. But it wouldn't hurt to have a little better idea of their reasons for lurking hereabouts.

He gave a warning squeeze to Red's muzzle that would keep the big horse quiet, then swiftly set about breaking camp and saddling up. He worked in silence save for the occasional creak of leather and the soft rustle of leaves underfoot.

The chore done, he led Red a little farther away, straining his eyes in the gloom to pick out the ground ahead of them. Leaving Red standing unmoving, he ghosted back toward the sounds of the strangers' camp. The murmur of voices and the shufflings of horses came to him. The scent of coffee and some kind of burned food made his nostrils flare.

He placed each foot with caution. Such sounds as he made could've passed for those of varmints, but he did his best not to make any at all. He slipped at last behind the wide bole of an old oak and crouched to peer through a tangle of intervening brush.

It took him a moment to make out the details of the scene before him. A good-sized fire had been built, and a handful of hard-edged men were lounging about, swigging at a whiskey bottle that was making the rounds. They'd apparently already devoured whatever food had been burned over the flames. Their horses were tethered beyond.

Stark wondered that he hadn't been roused sooner by their presence. The days of watchfulness must've dulled his senses.

He studied their stubbled faces in the uncertain firelight. He fancied he recognized one of them as a thief wanted in Oklahoma Territory. The others were strangers to him, but all had the stamp of lawless human predators.

"Reckon we'll find him?" one of them queried, and spat tobacco juice into the flames. "There's a whole passel of folks would like to get him in their sights."

"Shoot, he's got to be out here someplace," another responded. "We're as likely to find him as any of the rest of them."

"Unless some hombre's already bagged him," the first countered sourly.

Stark didn't harbor many doubts as to whom they were talking about. He scowled in the darkness. The whole prairie was crawling with gun trash like this looking to fill his hide with holes. Lucius Kincaid was totaling up a mighty big score to settle. Stark's muscles tensed. For a moment he had to fight the killing urge to pull both pistols and open up on this sorry crew. That would be five fewer killers hounding him.

He sucked in air through gritted teeth. He was on the verge of becoming as bloodthirsty as the men who hunted him. If that happened, Kincaid's score could be totaled even higher. Stark shook his head in stubborn refusal. He'd kill, but only when he had to. Only when there was no other trail to ride.

He'd seen enough. He eased himself back away from their camp.

"Hey, fellows!" a voice bawled unexpectedly out of the night. "There's a horse over here! A big sorrel like he's supposed to ride! Spread out! He could be around here somewhere!"

So there was one more of them, Stark understood instantly. Standing lookout, or prowling around on business of his own, he'd stumbled across Red and guessed the rest.

Commotion erupted in the camp. Stark used the noise to cover the sound of his charge toward the spot where he'd left the stallion. Ahead he could make out a dim human form. He exploded out of the bushes in a high leaping kick of savate, the brutal French art of foot fighting.

His driving boot rammed straight into the chest of the startled hardcase standing with drawn gun some yards distant from Red. The impact was akin to getting rammed by a railroad tie, and it bowled him over. His gun went sailing unfired from his fist. Stark rode him down, bowie knife already in his grip. Straddling his gasping victim, he hammered the hilt of the heavy knife down square between his eyes. The hardcase shuddered and went limp.

Shouting voices and sounds of crackling underbrush were converging on him. Sheathing the knife, Stark darted to Red. He led the sorrel farther into the woods. His mind was going at a gallop. With all of the man-hunters knowing he was nearby, he couldn't afford to run for it. If he did, they'd be breathing down his neck. Flight across the prairie would make him an easy target for their guns under the glaring stars. He'd have to deal with all of them, or he'd be dodging them the rest of the night with no relief in sight on the morrow. Better to deal with them now.

He slipped silently away from Red, leaving his saddle guns in their sheaths. They'd only get in his way for this type of work amid the trees and underbrush. He could hear several of the bunch crashing about. He halted, straining his ears, trying to get each of them located.

"Say your prayers, Peacemaker!" growled a voice behind him.

Stark felt his gut drop. He'd located one of them, all right, one who'd been smart enough to stay in one place and wait him out.

He had a second or less to react. As the hammer of a pistol clicked back, Stark crouched, leaped, and spun in a single straining burst of effort. He brought his leg snapping up and around in midair, using savate again. There was no chance for anything else. He had only the voice of the man behind him to aim for, and he prayed it was enough. It was. Like the end of a swinging singletree, his boot crashed into the side of the gunman's head. His gun lanced a roaring flame past Stark's body.

The force of the kick twisted Stark about. The gunman crumpled, and Stark hopped sidewise to regain his balance. He straightened, drained by his effort, his ears chiming from the blast of the gun.

He needed to move before the gunshot drew the others. At a crouch he darted into the brush. At breakneck speed, he ran for several yards, careless now in his haste to get clear.

The carelessness cost him. "Hold it, Stark," a surly voice ordered. "You're covered. I got a score to settle with you, and quick killing is too easy a way to do it."

Stark halted. His nerves screamed like barbed wire strung too taut. This sorry bunch was liable to be the death of him, he thought with despair. Like the other, this one was behind him, but he was too far away for any fancy kicks to drop him.

"Okay." Stark let his shoulders sag in what was almost real defeat. "You've got me. Look, I'm putting my hands behind me for the cuffs. Go ahead, snap them on."

"Cuffs?" the gunman's exclamation rang with disbelief. "I ain't no blamed lawman! I ain't going to cuff you! I'm going to—"

Before he could finish, Stark's fingers, under cover of the darkness, closed on the butt of the Marlin .38 double-action that rode concealed behind his gun belt at the small of his back. He drew it and fired like a trickshot artist without a mirror, again aiming by sound alone. Three times, rapid-fire, he pulled the trigger, then sidestepped and wheeled tightly about.

The stricken face of the gunman was grotesque in the gloom. At least one of the three blind shots had gone home. Coldly Stark shot again to be sure. He couldn't afford mercy at this juncture.

He didn't wait to see the man fall. Remotely he wondered what grudge his victim had held against him. He'd never know. Whatever it was, the gunman had come blessed close to paying it off.

Stark forced himself to move stealthily. His haste had nearly gotten him killed. At any moment he expected to feel the shock of a bullet or hear the snarl of another voice. He felt naked and vulnerable, as though he'd ventured out on the open prairie after all. Two times in not much over that many minutes, he'd let himself be blindsided. His heart battered his rib cage, and a brassy taste came to his mouth. Was this how it felt when a man finally lost his nerve?

He sank to one knee in the shelter of a towering bole and swapped the Marlin for the Colt .45. The Peacemaker. Its familiar heft steadied him. He'd beaten two dead drops, one without even drawing a gun. Whoever collected that bounty on him was blamed sure still going to have to earn it. He had a stretch of nerve left yet— enough to deal with these tinhorns.

He calculated there were six of them in all. Three were out of the fray, one permanently. The two he'd knocked out might be rejoining their compadres before much longer. He'd managed to lower the odds, but he had to end things fast before they once more increased against him.

He swiveled his head left and right, listening, scenting the breeze. Then he blinked in surprise. A flickering gleam of light shone through an interwoven matte work of branches and vines. Squinting, he could make out a dim form moving cautiously with one arm outstretched. A lighted lantern dangled from his fist.

Stark shook his head in disbelief. The loco fool was actually using a lantern to look for him! Stark parted the tangle of brush with the barrel of the .45 and lined it on the thick body behind the lantern. He eased back the hammer and let his finger tighten on the trigger.

Then he scowled with disgust. It was too much like shooting a dumb animal that had blundered into trouble because it didn't know any better. He lowered his sights a bit and finished squeezing the trigger. The .45 roared deafeningly and kicked his fist up. The lantern toter's leg buckled and he went down hollering. The lantern broke with a tinkle of glass. The flame flared brightly, then died away.

Stark lunged for other cover, feeling branches scrape at his face like clawed fingers. He heard return fire, but didn't spot the muzzle flashes. He fetched up in a shallow draw and hunkered down.

The echoes of the shots faded away. There were no more sounds from the lantern bearer. Likely, the shock of the leg wound had made him pass out.

Everybody was playing a waiting game now, Stark surmised. The hardcases were content to lay low until he came looking for them. *Not in the cards, boys,* he vowed grimly. *I'll make you come look for me.*

It took him a moment to get oriented, then he stalked through the woods like a hunting puma in the direction of their camp. He reached it and did a brief reconnoiter. The fire had died down some. None of the hardcases had returned. Their horses were shifting and snorting uneasily where they'd been tethered to a tie line stretched between two trees.

Stark crossed to the animals. Carefully he untied one and knotted its lead rope to a tree. The others observed him warily, rolling their eyes so the whites gleamed in the faint remaining glimmer of firelight. The shooting, the yells, and the smell of blood had made them jumpy. Stark circled behind them, clear of the glow of the fire. He was careful to stay out of range of their hind feet.

Once in place, he drew a deep breath, then expelled it in a loud shout. He waved his arms wildly and shouted some more. The line of horses erupted into a miniature rodeo of bucking broncs, held only by their tether rope. They neighed and whinnied frantically, their cries carrying eerily through the night. One of them lashed out backwards at Stark with high-flying hooves.

"He's fooling with the horses!" a man cried frantically from the forest. "Stop him!"

No horseman wanted to be left afoot in this country, particularly with a man-killer of Stark's caliber on a rampage. The threat to their mounts ought to bring the remaining pair on the run.

Swiftly Stark pulled the bowie and slashed the tether rope. Leaving their herd mate tied to the tree, the other five animals whirled and bolted into the woods. Stark was already moving around the perimeter of the campsite.

"They're getting away!" One of the hardcases burst out of the brush, gun in hand. His pard was a step behind him. Cursing, they drew up short as they saw the shadowy shapes of the fleeing horses disappearing into the darkness.

''There's one horse left!'' the bigger one blurted.

''The devil with that! Where's Stark?''

They both went rigid with realization of just how big of a mistake they'd made.

''Right here, boys,'' Stark answered from behind them. ''Drop those guns and grab some night.''

They stood like totems for a long ragged moment. ''There's more of us,'' the big one blustered.

''There *were* more of you,'' Stark corrected softly. ''And believe me, fellows, I'd rather kill you than stand here palavering.'' It was almost the truth.

Both guns hit the dirt.

''Now, down on your hands and knees.''

Grudgingly, they obeyed. Stark moved closer.

''I'm feeling merciful tonight,'' he drawled, ''although heaven knows I've got plenty of reason to be riled, what with your sorry outfit disturbing my sleep and trying to bag me like I was some renegade lobo with a price on his head.''

''We wasn't—'' the larger one started to protest.

Stark cut him off coldly. ''Shut up and listen hard. If you make it through this, don't ever even entertain the notion of bucking me again, bounty or no bounty. I'll whittle you into sawdust, then grind you into the ground. You can give your pards and anybody else who cares to listen that same message. Savvy?''

While they were still nodding like a couple of trained dogs, Stark stepped in fast and struck twice with the barrel of the .45, dropping them senseless on their faces. He didn't like using a gun in that fashion, but it was fast and efficient. Wyatt Earp himself had been an old hand at it back in his town-taming days.

Stark acted swiftly. He collected their pistols, ejected the cylinders, and chucked them and the frames in opposite directions as far as he could into the brush. Then, kneeling, he drew the bowie and slashed at their boots, careless if he nicked the flesh underneath in the process. The keen blade sawed through the worn leather. Stark tossed the tattered footwear aside. Let them try walking out of here without their boots, or catching their horses if they could. Either way, it'd make for a good lesson.

He repeated the process on the three he'd left alive in the brush. He used the wounded man's kerchief to tie off the bleeding from his wound. One of the other pair needed a second kick to flatten him again.

Prudence would be proud of him, he reflected wryly. He'd put six foes out of action, and had only had to kill one of them in doing it. He didn't think any of this hapless crew would be coming after him again. He reckoned they'd learned that they were outclassed.

But there'd be more of them, and not all of them would be this inept.

He recalled the rumors back at the Ark that Gundance was out to collect the bounty. If Trowbridge had been among this bunch, Stark might not have cause to be feeling so cocky about now, he acknowledged bleakly. But a wolf never ran with the town dogs. And the wild stallion he'd seen on the prairie wouldn't expect his mares to fight his battles for him. If Trowbridge was in this game—and Stark figured it was a good bet that he was—he wouldn't want to share the reward or the glory that came from being the man who outgunned the Peacemaker.

Stark went back to the camp and collected the lone horse he'd left tethered there. It was a rangy buckskin gelding. Now another bounty could be posted on him for being a horse thief. But the beast seemed a fair trade for the lives of the hardcases. Having a spare mount to spell Red would make traveling a bit easier on Stark and the sorrel alike.

He took the best of the saddles and slapped it on the buckskin. The gelding bared his square teeth in disapproval, but didn't get really ornery about it, Stark was pleased to note.

Almost regretfully, he employed the bowie further on the remaining saddles. A shame to ruin good gear, but if the hardcases did catch their horses, he figured riding bareback would slow them down plenty if they set out on his trail.

Astride the gelding, and leading Red, he headed out. He would still make a fine target on the prairie, so he stayed with the course of the stream, moving along the outer edge of the woods where the going was easier.

The stars had swung a long way across the sky, and he'd put a good distance between himself and the hardcases when he finally stopped and made camp again.

If Trowbridge wanted a chance against him one-on-one, he promised himself silently, he'd see that the bounty hunter got it.

Chapter Seven

" "Telegram for you, Miss McKay."

Prudence looked up at the teenage lad who had just entered her office. She recognized him as a courier for the telegraph company. Eagerness quickened her heartbeat as she rose from her chair and rounded her desk.

"Here, I'll sign for it."

The youth looked a little flustered at the speed with which she scribbled her name and passed him a coin. It was too much of a tip, but she didn't care at the moment.

She used her fingernails to open the flimsy telegraph office envelope, not even bothering with the letter opener within arm's reach on her desk. She paused as she realized the courier had not moved.

"Yes?"

He blushed and swallowed hard. "You, uh, want me to wait for a reply?" There was a worshipful gleam in his eye that might have more to do with his reluctance to leave than any desire to be of service.

She bestowed her best friendly smile on him. "No, that won't be necessary."

"Uh, well, okay."

As he backed slowly out of the office, it occurred to her that he seemed to have valued her smile more than her generous tip.

Then she put such reflections aside as she ran her eyes over the printed lines of the missive. She read it again to be sure, then squeezed her eyes tightly shut for a moment. "Thank heaven," she murmured reverently.

The telegram was the result of the only action she had been able to think of that might help James Stark get out from under the illicit bounty hanging over him. And she was helping him, she confirmed to herself resolutely. Even if, when he found out, he wouldn't think so. Meddling is what he would call it. Or, more likely, butting into his affairs.

It didn't matter. She had felt compelled to do something, not only for his safety, but also to stop him from going on some killing rampage that he would surely regret, and that might have terrible legal repercussions for him. And personal ones for her, she was honest enough to admit to herself. In his savage rage over being marked for murder, James Stark might be driven to actions that would forever mar her relationship with him, however nebulous that relationship was.

Certainly she didn't—couldn't—love him. Any fleeting thoughts to the contrary at one time or another had only been juvenile girlish notions that she should've long outgrown. She didn't love him, she was certain; but she did care deeply for him as a friend and sometime social companion. That was it; there was nothing more to what lay between them.

Still, waiting for the response to her inquiries, and praying for Jim's safety, had been the only things that had enabled her to carry on through the long frustrating days that had passed since attorney James Mathers had come personally with word of his encounter with the Peacemaker.

He had certainly gone out of his way to see her, and she had noticed that he seemed very interested in her reaction to his tale.

She knew him in passing as a rather pleasant and reasonably handsome young barrister who was rumored to have killed at least one man in a gunfight that had been forced upon him. She had always enjoyed his company when their work had brought them into contact with one another.

Absurdly, she found herself wondering what he had said to Stark concerning her. And what might Stark have said to him? She had struggled to remember anything she might've said to Mathers about Jim that he could've repeated, until she decided firmly that such matters were of no consequence.

Still, it would've been interesting to listen in on the conversation between the two men.

She had paid rapt attention to his account of the affair in the notorious Ark. Sensations of relief, pride, and some other unfathomable feeling had mingled in her breast upon learning that Stark had used no more force than was absolutely necessary to learn what he wanted to know and escape the men seeking his life.

But the grim resolve in his promise to take a bounty of his own had chilled the marrow of her bones. She fancied she could all but hear the unyielding tone of his voice, and picture the hard set of his square jaw as he'd uttered the foreboding words.

Mathers had already recounted his tale to Evett Nix, in accordance with his instructions from Stark. She was a little miffed that Jim's message had been to the lawman and not to her. But she'd made her views on his vendetta clear to Jim, so it was no wonder that he chose to send word of his progress to Nix.

She had hurried to Nix's office. "I've put some men on it," the U.S. Marshal had told her. "We'll see if we can get some verification." He broke off under Prudence's level gaze, and shifted his shoulders uncomfortably. "That's all I can do," he said a trifle defensively. "Remember, my powers are limited in the Indian Lands. I can't just go barging in willy-nilly. And James refused to cooperate with me. I need something more to go on than rumors from a dive as disreputable as the Ark."

"Thank you, Marshal," she said icily. "If I discover anything else of interest, I'll be sure to inform you." On that note, she had turned and swept out of his office.

Remembering that scene, and the days, stretching as long as the wait for a jury's verdict, that had passed since then, she felt a tremor of excitement now as she donned a shawl and left her office.

Outside, she hurried toward the Herriott Building. Her pace was quite unseemly, but there were times when one had to disregard the proprieties. She realized she had crumpled the telegram a bit, so tightly had she been clutching it in her small fist. She loosened her grip and tried to smooth the sheet against her dress without slackening her stride.

She was slightly breathless when she reached the Herriott. She slowed her gait as she ascended the stairs to the marshal's office. She even forced herself to take a moment to regain her composure and straighten her hair.

As usual, she had little trouble in gaining access to Nix's presence, although the marshal's look was carefully neutral as he rose to greet her. "Prudence. What can I do—"

She extended the telegram, feeling her lips tremble with her effort to keep from smiling triumphantly. "Read this."

Still eyeing her warily, he reached across his neatly organized desk to accept the sheet. His brow furrowed as he read. She could tell he went over it twice to be sure he had absorbed it fully.

When he lifted his head, his face was still expressionless. "Your father?" he inquired.

Prudence nodded wordlessly. Judge Uriah McKay was a renowned jurist in Kansas. He wielded subtle power and had unlikely connections as far away as the nation's capital itself. Prudence had called on that power to be wielded, and for those connections to be used in her relentless search to find a weakness in the man who had the temerity to pass his own private death sentence on James Stark.

She could contain herself no longer. "Lucius Kincaid is wanted in New York!" she announced with heartfelt satisfaction. She went on, repeating what Nix had already gleaned from the telegram, and adding other information she had acquired in her investigations. "He killed his business partner and absconded with a great deal of cash, some of which was state money, on loan from the U.S. government when it happened."

She was still hazy on the details of the convoluted business dealings of Kincaid and his luckless partner, but she did understand the legal consequences for Kincaid.

"There's a warrant for Kincaid's arrest," she went on rapidly. The governor of New York is making a formal request to the governor of Oklahoma Territory and the president of the United States that the warrant be served in Indian Lands by the federal officers responsible for law enforcement in the Territories. The supporting documents are on their way here!"

"I don't need to wait for that," Nix said flatly. "You've gotten me what I needed to be able to act. Good job!" He was smiling.

"Then you'll send some of your deputies after Kincaid?" Prudence couldn't conceal her elation. She hadn't been certain how Nix would react to having her try to help him do his job.

But if he bore her any ill will, it certainly wasn't evident in the affirmative nod he gave her in reply, or in his manner as he strode to the door of his office and barked orders.

"Have a seat, Miss McKay." He became more formal when he turned to address her. "We'll have some action in just a few moments if you'd care to wait."

She cared to do so. Fidgeting, she seated herself in one of the guest chairs. She sat on the very edge of the cushion, her back as straight as though she was trying to pass a posture test from the young ladies' schools of her youth.

Nix busied himself studying a large map of the Territories that covered most of one wall of his office. "Right about here," he declared after a few moments, and jabbed a spot on the map with an emphatic finger.

"What?" Prudence exclaimed in a tone that was so high pitched it embarrassed her.

"Kincaid's stronghold," Nix explained over his shoulder. "As near as we can estimate, this is its location."

Prudence popped out of the chair and crossed swiftly to his side. Her spirits sagged a little as she calculated the distance between the territorial capital and the remote spot on the map. She noted bleakly that there were no indications of railroads or communities anywhere in the immediate vicinity.

"That's a long way," she said with a dispirited sigh.

Nix nodded thoughtfully. "If he's headed there, Stark's likely to be staying to cover and taking his time so as to avoid discovery by bounty hunters. He may not have had time to reach there yet."

Prudence felt her hopes stir. She tried to imagine Jim traveling warily through the vast hostile area portrayed on the map. With sudden vividness, she recalled those days when the two of them had journeyed in just such a fashion, on the run from the outlaw gang that had kidnapped her. It had been Stark who had rescued her and carried her to safety.

There had been a peculiar bond that developed between them during that time. She had come to know him and to understand that many of her preconceived notions of him as a cold-blooded mercenary had been very, very wrong.

She had felt an involuntary shiver race over her, and hoped Nix didn't notice. She turned impatiently to the door. Her feelings for Jim Stark remained confused. At times she wished she'd never met him. Her emotions always seemed to be in a disconcerting whirl these days. This present endeavor on Jim's behalf was a perfect example of the trouble he'd caused her. He was simply too stubborn for his own good. And for hers. Once this business concerning Lucius Kincaid was finished, she'd be better off washing her hands of Jim Stark for good.

At that moment two men stepped into the office. "You wanted to see us, Evett?" the older one in the lead inquired.

Nix had certainly called in the best for this job, Prudence realized. A thirty-year veteran of law enforcement in the West, Heck Thomas had a sterling reputation as a fighting man of courage and honor. Showing some age now, with gray beginning to lighten his mustache, he still had the lean build of a horseman. Ivory-handled six-shooters rode his belt. He didn't wear a badge. A polite acknowledgment came from him as his level gray eyes fell on Prudence.

"Come on in, both of you," Nix invited, leaving off his study of the map.

Thomas's companion followed him into the room, looming tall and strong behind him. And as she got a good look at him, Prudence's heart gave a quite uncharacteristic flutter, despite herself.

The stranger was much younger than Thomas, closer to her own age, Prudence assessed automatically. And he was big, with a stalwart build, an easygoing manner, and an appealing boyish handsomeness. He wore range gear, and a standard deputy's star was affixed to the front of his freshly scrubbed blue shirt. A single gun was holstered on an unornamented belt. He doffed his hat as he came through the door.

Prudence found herself watching his eyes as they lighted on her. She saw not the crude desire she had half expected, and so often received. Instead, there was the fully respectful appreciation of a well-mannered man for an attractive lady. He dropped his gaze quickly, as if genuinely embarrassed to have been caught staring. Prudence realized she had been staring some too. She was sure she had never encountered this intriguing U.S. Deputy before.

"Heck, I think you know Miss Prudence McKay," Nix said by way of introductions. "Miss McKay, this is Stand Garner, one of our newest deputies. He's from up in the Dakotas. Did some law enforcement work up there before coming down here to see how it's really done."

As a rule, Prudence preferred to shake hands when she met someone for the first time, be they male or female. It made that first contact more personal, and could be disconcerting for men expecting a shy, wilting female—a reaction that Prudence often found worthwhile in the legal arena.

But as Stand Garner stepped forward, she felt suddenly flustered and contented herself with as business-like a nod as she could manage. She sensed that she was the one who would become disconcerted if her hand touched his.

Furiously, she remonstrated with herself as Nix directed them to chairs. She was reacting like some silly schoolgirl seeing a comely boy for the first time. Usually such embarrassing episodes were reserved for James Stark. And here she was feeling all fluttery about a young man who, she was certain, was a mere youth in experience and worldliness next to James.

But was that all bad? And why should James even enter into it? There was nothing serious between her and Stark. She owed him this current effort to keep him out of the trouble he had created for himself, but she had already decided she'd be better off without his presence in her life.

So why did it matter whether he ever had an inkling of the spontaneous spark that had leaped between her and Stand Garner? Her emotions were none of James's business. And there was no denying the immediate undeniable appeal the big young deputy stirred in her.

This wasn't the time for such thoughts, she told herself, and became aware of Nix recounting to the deputies the newest developments regarding the bounty on the head of James Stark.

"I've heard tell of Kincaid," Thomas mused aloud. "He's supposed to live like a king back up in his fancy hacienda. Likes his privacy, the man does, and he's willing to shell out a pretty penny hiring gunmen to ensure it."

Garner appeared to be paying close attention to the other men, but Prudence fancied that his eyes slid briefly over to her. She dropped her gaze demurely.

"With the information Miss McKay has so capably obtained, we have enough cause to enter the Indian Lands and take Kincaid into immediate custody," Nix continued. "That should squelch this bounty nonsense once and for all. Heck, I want you to round up half a dozen good men and bring Kincaid in. Take Stand here with you. It's a fine opportunity for him to learn the ropes. Any questions?''

Heck shook his head in a slow negative. In terms of practical experience he far outclassed Nix, Prudence knew. And the younger marshal had relied heavily on Thomas's advice in manning and organizing his force of deputies.

"It'll be a pleasure to lend a hand to Jim Stark. This business about the bounty has stuck in my craw ever since I first heard of it,'' Heck drawled. ''We'll be sure to spread the word the bounty's been canceled. We'll also do our best to bring Stark back alive and well.'' With this final comment he glanced at Prudence, as if his words should have some special significance to her.

She maintained a neutral expression.

Garner had been leaning forward, forearms on his knees, twirling his hat absently in his fingers. He straightened some now. ''I'd heard of Stark all the way back to the Dakotas,'' he commented. ''Is he really as good as all that?''

"Good enough so that he just might get to Kincaid first and save us the trouble, despite having a pack of gunhounds out for his blood.'' Thomas smiled mirthlessly beneath his graying mustache.

"I have it on strong authority that Lance Trowbridge has joined the hunt for Stark,'' Nix said.

Garner sat up even straighter. His hazel eyes grew brighter. ''Well, now, is that a fact? Gundance himself. The master bounty hunter.''

Heck Thomas snorted. ''Don't be playing his game, kid. If you come up against him, take my advice and drop him with a load of buckshot before he ever has a chance to make his two-bit challenge.''

"He's that good?'' Garner demanded with avid interest.

"Maybe better than Stark,'' Thomas muttered, then looked sorry he had spoken the words.

Nix didn't pursue the subject. "He regarded Prudence with inquiring eyes. "Satisfied with my arrangements, Prudence?''

"Yes,'' she said primly. "Except for one thing. I want to accompany Deputy Thomas and his posse.''

Nix's jaw dropped. Heck Thomas gave another snort. Garner gaped at her.

All of them sputtered similar protests, but it was Nix who rose to his feet and overrode his subordinates. "That's loco! It'd be too dangerous! I can't place you at that kind of risk!''

"You wouldn't be placing me,'' Prudence countered calmly. "I'd be placing myself. I insist on going. Remember, without me, you wouldn't even have the wherewithal to arrest Kincaid.''

"But why, for Pete's sake?''

She had carefully marshaled her arguments, exactly as she would have done in preparing a case for the courtroom. "I'm the only one who can stop Jim Stark from killing Lucius Kincaid, short of using force,'' she said emphatically, then pressed on with every fragment of persuasive skill that her training, experience, and temperament had given her.

"Listen. You don't want the Peacemaker on some kind of rampage going after the man who has set him up to be killed. You don't want a bloodbath, with hired

guns, would-be bounty hunters, and maybe innocent by-
standers—including members of the tribes—getting
killed. And you know that's what could happen. You've
seen the kind of damage Jim can do when he has the
incentive. Remember the Garland gang? Jim wiped them
out almost single-handedly. And he destroyed Randall
Burke's operation in No-Man's-Land. He might do the
same thing to Lucius Kincaid. Even Deputy Thomas just
said as much!

"Think about it! How would it look if the man two
governors and the U.S. government are requesting you
apprehend is killed by the very man he conspired to
murder, all under your jurisdiction? How will that look
on your record?

"I think I can stop that from happening," she rushed
on. "But only if I can reach Jim in time. I can persuade
him to let the law run its course. If your men get in
Jim's way, I can't answer for the consequences. A head-
on clash between the Peacemaker and U.S. Deputies
would be disastrous!"

She was breathing hard with the passion of her ora-
tory, and she paused to draw breath and let her words
sink in. She had raised the specters of innocent deaths,
widespread violence, and political repercussions. To that
mix she had added an implied threat to Nix's career.
This last, she admitted, smacked of underhandedness,
but the danger to Nix was very real, just the same.

And she wasn't done yet.

"As for my safety, I can ride and shoot. I've proven
that, as you know. And a lady couldn't be safer than
with six U.S. Deputy Marshals." She dropped her air
of courtroom professionalism, looking at Nix with

pleading eyes, putting it all on a personal level now. "Jim is your friend, Evett. He's mine too. We can't let him throw his life away on some foolish vendetta. I can even help your men find him. I know how he thinks, maybe better than anyone. And he won't be so prone to resort to violence if I'm present. Please, Evett!"

She had presented her best case. She prayed the verdict would be in her favor.

But Nix, she saw, appeared unconvinced. He opened his mouth as though to speak, and her heart sank.

Heck Thomas cleared his throat. "The lady's making some sense," he opined laconically.

"We'll look after her, Marshal!" Garner vowed.

She sensed his eagerness to have her along, and was pleased by his support.

Nix exhaled tiredly and regarded all of them.

"You're a persuasive woman, Miss McKay," he said at last. "That was as well argued a case as I've ever heard in a court of law by you or any other attorney. Giving in to you goes contrary to my better judgment. But I'm also aware that you're a woman who knows her own mind, and I have a sneaking suspicion you plan to go along whether I give my approval or not. If you showed up at their camp once my men were out in the Lands, they couldn't very well afford to turn around and bring you back, could they?"

Prudence suspected her blush gave him ample confirmation of the truth of his analysis.

Nix shook his head in exasperation. "May the Good Lord and your father forgive me. You can go."

Chapter Eight

When he first spotted the six riders far behind him, Stark felt a twinge of irritation. He'd managed to dodge any further manhunters since tangling with the bunch by the creek. But now this pack seemed to have hit on his trail.

But they were far enough away to be little more than an annoyance. Still, he'd rather have encountered them late in the day rather than now in the midmorning hours. The sun, attended by cottony clouds, was edging its way up the blue dome of the sky.

Returning to Red and the gelding, Stark mounted the hardcase's horse, with his field glasses slung around his neck. With two horses under him, he shouldn't have much trouble leaving his pursuers far behind him.

He held the animals' pace to a steady gallop as the sun inched higher. When he finally halted and used the glasses without dismounting, he drew a breath of satisfaction. Nothing showed between him and the far horizon. A notch-winged vulture floated hopefully far overhead. Other than that, he might've been alone on the whole sea of grass.

He kept moving at an easy trot, choosing to stay on the gelding. The buckskin had proven a good choice. It had plenty of bottom.

To be safe, he stopped after another mile and lifted the glasses to look. He lowered them sharply, squinted with his naked eyes, then lifted them and looked again. An icy serpent slithered down his spine. The handful of riders was still back there, and they were closer than when he'd looked before.

But were they the same riders? It seemed to him as though one of them had worn a white Stetson. It had shone plainly in the sunlight. Nothing like that could be seen among this bunch.

He had a suspicion then, but he put it aside. What mattered at the moment was outdistancing them. Grimly, he put heels to the gelding, pushing the pace to a league-eating gallop just short of a run.

For two miles he held to the gallop, then another at a lope, before he checked his back trail. It was clear.

Only slightly relieved, he moved on. The same, or another, vulture still floated lazily far overhead, like a tiny scrap of ash caught in the wind.

In a half hour he reined up and surveyed his back trail again. Somehow he was hardly surprised to see the now familiar grouping of distant mounted figures coming steadily in his wake. Stark shook his head. They were yet out of range for most saddle guns, but their relentless pursuit was unnerving. No single bunch of horsemen should've been able to hang so stubbornly on his trail without wearing their horses out. These seemed tireless.

He put a ridge between them and slanted off at an angle. Maybe they'd keep right on going and pass him by. His hopes faded when he next used the glasses. They were still dogging his trail, and they'd cut across the angle to gain on him even more. A spot of white gleamed atop one rider's head.

He was certain then, and his gut coiled as tight as a prodded rattler. At least three teams of horsemen, maybe more, were riding in relays to keep him moving. And they had a pretty fair tracker among them who, even in the thick buffalo grass, had picked up his trail when he veered off his original course. As one team tired, the next, following at a slower pace, could take up the chase, while the first group loafed at a slower rate behind them until their horses were rested. The process could be repeated almost indefinitely, especially if three teams were involved.

Three or more crews meant a good fifteen to twenty men. He hadn't expected the saloon sweepings who had been plaguing him to be able to get that organized. A single leader and a kind of lynch-mob mentality could hold them together for a spell, he reckoned, but problems might arise when it came time to split the bounty. For now, though, each of them would be caught up in the hunt, and likely figuring on somehow claiming the lion's share of the money for himself once it was theirs. The prospect of a falling-out offered little comfort. Conflict among his pursuers after the bounty had been earned sure wouldn't do him any good. . . .

He let the horses run, swinging in a wide arc to get well clear of the pursuing teams. He was being driven off his course, but there was no help for that now. He'd have to make up the lost distance when he'd evaded them.

If he evaded them.

The sun was high enough to heat up the landscape.

The gelding was sweating hard. And even Red, burdened by only a saddle, would be beginning to feel the effects of their pace. Features taut, Stark pushed them on.

Far off to his left a bobbing irregularity on the horizon caught his eye. He leaned in that direction, his eyes narrowed, and he growled deep in his throat. Yet another crew of horsemen, or maybe one of the groups who'd earlier been on his back trail, was riding hard to intercept him. Frustration and anger tensed his muscles. He was being chased and harried like a renegade bronc. He recollected the wild stallion he'd seen days before. Had it ever been run in this fashion?

Time to switch mounts. The gelding was near to being played out. He'd need Red's speed and endurance to pull clear of this trap before it closed.

With a tug of the reins, he urged Red alongside the straining gelding without slowing the buckskin's pace. In a moment the two animals were running neck and neck, scarcely a foot separating them. Stark scanned the ground ahead. He could see no obstacles or pitfalls.

Timing his moves, he kicked his feet free of the stirrups and swung his leg over Red's saddle. Then, like a trick rider, he levered himself smoothly off the gelding and onto Red.

He felt his seat settle firmly into the saddle, and in that same moment the buckskin faltered, its stride breaking. Stark had seen that effect too many times to have any doubts about what had happened. The gelding had taken a bullet. It had been hit, and hit hard, by a shot fired from so far off that he might never hear the report over the beat of the horses' hooves.

The buckskin was going down, and when it did it would drag Red with it, hurling Stark himself from the saddle, or thrusting him beneath tumbling horses and flailing hooves. His hand streaked for the bowie. He ripped it from its sheath and slashed with an upward jerk of his arm. The honed steel of the reverse edge on the big blade sheered cleanly through the taut reins linking the two animals together.

The stricken gelding went head over heels in a wrenching tumble. Had he been a fraction of a second later in his flying remount, Stark would've gone with him. Red staggered, then caught his stride. One eye rolled wildly back at Stark.

Far ahead, rising like an island, was a rugged butte, its sides scarred with red dirt where no vegetation had found purchase. Rocky outcrops jutted in profusion. Stark pointed Red's muzzle toward it and let him have his head. One way or another he was going to have to deal with this misbegotten army of bounty hunters. The butte was the only terrain that offered any sort of a place to fort up.

They were after him from two sides. Red's full speed let him pull ahead of the pack to the rear. The crew off on the left was closing the gap as they sought to cut him off from the butte.

The shot that had dropped the buckskin could've been intended for him. It had been fired from a heavy-caliber, long-range weapon like an old-fashioned Sharps Big Fifty. Which meant that he might still be in danger. He rode bent low in the saddle to make a smaller target and cut the push of the wind.

But there were no more shots. Whoever the sharpshooter was, he had given up slinging lead in hopes of intercepting him before he reached the butte.

It loomed ahead of him, and he scanned it desperately for a route up its steep face. His eyes caught a trace of track snaking up to the summit—likely a path worn by wandering cattle or antelope.

Off to his left he could hear the shouts of the pack cutting in on him. Gunfire began to pop futilely. He was going to beat them, he could tell, but they were pressing a mite too close for comfort. Pulling his Colt, he threw lead at them for the sake of discouragement.

A quick sideward glance showed them to be slowing a bit. Then Stark only had time to concentrate on putting Red up the steep trail etched in the red dirt and sandstone of the butte's face.

Angry yells followed his ascent, and a rifle bullet screamed off an outcropping as he passed by it. Red's driving hooves sprayed miniature landslides of dirt and stone behind them. Stark saw sparks fly as one shod hoof met stone.

With a last surge, Red crested the butte, legs trembling from his effort at running flat-out up a near-vertical surface. Stark hurled himself from the saddle, holding the shotgun in one fist, the rifle in the other. He whirled to look back at the riders clustering at the foot of the escarpment. Two of them had started to urge their horses up the trail. The animals were balking as they failed to find good purchase beneath their hooves. A couple of bullets sang past Stark's ears. Some of the cooler hands were trying their luck at marksmanship from their standing horses.

Stark sank to one knee, laying the rifle aside. He

tucked the shotgun tight to his shoulder, sighted down
its barrel at the mass of men and animals sixty feet below him, and cut loose, levering and firing. The shotgun's blasts ran together in a single ongoing roar as he
emptied all four loads—buckshot and slugs—down into
their midst.

In the aftermath of the barrage, they scattered like
chickens chased by a coyote. Blinking through the
smoke, Stark saw two men and one horse were down.
The horse lurched to its feet and hightailed it at a limp-
ing gallop. Neither man moved.

Stark snatched up the rifle, but resisted the urge to
start picking the others off the backs of their horses as
they fled. Maybe they'd had enough. The other group
was pulling to a halt some eight hundred yards out.

Hastily, he saw to Red, moving him far enough back
from the edge so he couldn't be targeted from below.
There were a few stunted trees and some sparse grass
on the acre-size tabletop of the butte, but no water. He
had expected none, but it meant he and the stallion
would likely have dry throats before this was over. If
they were still alive.

He returned to what he thought of as the front of the
butte, which he had ascended. Several jumbles of boul-
ders offered good cover. The shoulders of the small
mesa weren't as steep as the face, but they'd still slow
a rider considerably, especially if he knew a ready gun
was waiting for him at the top.

Stark didn't take time to survey the rear of his sanctuary. From the shelter of an outcropping, he used his
field glasses to study the scene out on the plain. His
besiegers had retreated out of easy rifle range. Another

group had joined the first two, he saw, so his estimate as to their tactics and numbers hadn't been far off.

Some kind of a confab was going on. They were probably debating strategy. He took the opportunity to assess them a little more closely, then shook his head in disgust. For the most part they looked to be a sorry lot of saddle tramps, owlhoots, and drifters, forged for the moment into a ragtag army bent on lifting his scalp. He counted seventeen of them.

He couldn't pull out until Red had regained his strength. And once off the mesa he'd fall prey to their relay tactics again. He could only hope to hold them until nightfall, and then try to leave his stronghold and elude them in the darkness. Which meant, at the very least, waiting here through several hours of heat, frustration, and danger.

He reloaded the shotgun and affixed the telescopic sight to the rifle. He was well enough stocked on ammo. Loads for the rifle and shotgun were in the bandoliers crisscrossing his chest. The loops of his gun belt were filled with shells for the .45. He had more with his gear in his saddlebags.

Eight hundred yards away, out on the plain, it looked as though they were making plans to try something. Stark employed the glasses, then stiffened as he focused on one of their number he'd missed spotting before.

Even from a distance there was no mistaking the lean buckskinned form of the backwoods wolfer he had last seen slouching against the wall at the Ark in Purcell. The barbaric wolf skull dangling at his waist was plainly visible. Stark fancied he caught a whiff of the hider's stench carried on some vagrant breeze. The wolfer was toting the Sharps Big Fifty rifle.

Here, Stark reckoned, was the answer to who had tracked him down across all the miles of grassland. In the feral shape of the distant figure he could read the predatory spirit of the born hunter. Like the wolves he stalked, he'd be nigh unshakable once he got on a trail.

How he had attracted or organized the riffraff siding him, Stark couldn't guess. Maybe they were just curs following along in hopes of a few scraps when the lobo made his kill.

Stark reached for the big rifle, but when he got the scope to his eye, the wolfer was no longer in view. Scowling, Stark lowered the weapon.

The band of men was spreading out in a ragged line. Stark fingered the rifle. It was a good piece, a Winchester 1886 Sporting Rifle, lever-action 50–110 express, with an eight-shot magazine. He'd had it fitted with a special-order, thirty-inch octagonal barrel.

It amounted to a repeating buffalo gun, with all the range and power of the old Sharps the wolfer favored. But whereas the Sharps needed to be reloaded after each shot, the Sporting Rifle could keep firing until the magazine ran dry. If such a weapon had been available to the buffalo hunters in the old days, Stark reflected darkly, the herds of buffalo would've disappeared even more quickly from the range than they actually had. For man-killing at a distance, the rifle had no peer.

But, Stark realized, as with the hardcases by the creek, he didn't want to kill any more members of this rabble than he had to. He persisted in thinking of them as dupes, puppets in the scheming hands of Lucius Kincaid. The wolfer was a different matter, but these poor fools lining up to rush him would be nothing but cannon fodder.

Then he set his jaw tightly. Some of them still might have to die before the rest gave up the blood scent they followed.

Chapter Nine

Mounted, they came across the rangeland in a ragged skirmish line, yelling and shooting. Some fired their guns uselessly into the air. Others flung lead futilely at the butte.

They were going to need some discouraging, Stark decided. He sighted and pulled the trigger of the Sporting Rifle. It bucked and roared and spit a piece of lead as big as the end of his thumb. Far out there, the hat of the centermost rider in the line skipped from his head.

Stark shifted aim through the wreathing smoke to the rider next in line. Again the cannon in his hands roared, and the hombre's sombrero was snatched from his head as if by a violent gust of wind.

Stark changed positions, reloading as he moved. He had ample cover along the lip of the butte. Through the rifle's scope he viewed the results of his target practice.

It had taken a moment or two for the sound of the shots to reach them, and for them to realize what had happened. The line came to a straggling halt, and some of the riders bunched up. They would've made a dandy group of tartets if he was feeling bloodthirsty, Stark mused.

Apparently they figured the long-range shooting must've been a fluke, or else the result of a poor aim.

They weren't discouraged. The line re-formed and came charging across the prairie again.

Stark sighed. They hadn't taken the hint. Some folks were just plain stubborn, or dumb. He used the scope, calculating the wind and the speed of their charge. Seven hundred yards now, and closing in.

Grudgingly, Stark squeezed the trigger. He didn't wait to see the results of his shot, but lowered the barrel from its recoil, shifted it to the next rider, and fired again. He tried a third target, but as he pulled the trigger he saw the rider veer wildly, and understood that a re-action to his first two shots was setting in. He knew he'd missed his third.

He gathered himself to crab sidewise to a new posi-tion, but before he could move, a miniature cannonball seemed to strike the rock beside his face. Chips of stone flew.

Automatically he ducked and rolled. He'd stayed in one place too long and let his powder smoke target him for the same sharpshooter who'd dropped the gelding. He had no doubt it was the wolfer with his Sharps.

Letting himself be spotted was an amateur's stunt, but he'd figured none of the riders would be able to pinpoint him and return fire that fast. He still reckoned he was right, which meant the wolfer had been hunkered down somewhere waiting for him to shoot. Likely he'd been surprised at Stark's rate of fire and his accuracy at long range. That might've slowed his reaction time. Still, it'd been deuced fine shooting.

Warily, Stark edged his head up for a look-see. Only seconds had passed since the first of his three shots. Two riders were down, and the skirmish line had reversed course, its members riding hard to get some distance between themselves and their deadly prey.

All this Stark saw in a flashing glance. And he saw something else, a puff of smoke arising from behind a tiny ripple of ground near where the charge had first started. Instantly he cranked the lever and pumped two shots at the distant point. The heavy slugs shredded grass and punched up clods of earth, but his trained eye saw no sign of a solid hit. The wolfer must've already snaked to a different position.

Stark did the same, then popped up long enough to empty the magazine after the retreating riders. He wasn't trying to score hits, just to put the fear of the devil in them.

Hunched down in yet another position, he thumbed shells from one bandolier and fed them into the rifle. He felt a stinging on his cheek. His sweat had found its way to a tiny cut opened by a piece of rock. He sleeved at it impatiently.

The riders were regrouping out of easy range for even the Sporting Rifle. They weren't giving up, he realized with disappointment. He could spot neither hide nor hair of the wolfer.

Some kind of palaver seemed to be going on, and he risked slipping back from the lip of the plateau's rim. Legging it to Red, he snagged one of the canteens from his saddle and poured some water in his hat. The sorrel snuffled it gratefully. Stark had a long swig himself. He swished it around to keep his mouth moist for as long as possible, then swallowed.

Swiftly he scouted the rear of the butte. It dropped away steeply, but an active man could scale it easily enough. Stark repositioned Red closer to that side, hoping the stallion would give him warning of anybody trying to come in through the back door.

Something was up when he once more regained a vantage point at the front of the escarpment. He watched gaugingly. The afternoon sun was hot, and various itches were making themselves felt beneath his clothes. He ignored them.

A scattering of men with long guns edged forward on foot. Kneeling, they began to throw lead at the rim of the mesa. After a couple of shots they'd scuttle a few yards and reposition themselves. Some of the bullets plugged themselves weakly into the face of the butte, but for the most part the shooters were too far off to do much damage. Their fire only served to make Stark keep his head down.

That's all he figured it was supposed to do. Pulling back from the edge, he stood to get a clear view of the surrounding plains. Sure enough, through his field glasses, he spotted a trio of horsemen riding hard as they swung out in a wide arc that would bring them around to the vulnerable back side of his refuge. The ineffectual fire from the rest of the rabble was intended to keep him from spotting their flanking maneuver.

His face intent, Stark moved as close as he dared to the rim of one of the butte's shoulders. He sank to one knee behind a chest-high boulder that served as a rest for his rifle. The trio of riders were little more than specks to the naked eye. Even through the telescopic sight, they looked like distant child's toys.

Stark took his time sighting. This would be a long shot. He had to lead his target and allow for droppage of the heavy bullet as well. He wouldn't be aiming at the lead rider, but rather, above the the spot where he calculated the horseman would be when the bullet had had time to cover the intervening distance.

He lifted his head to swipe his forearm across his brow and squeeze his eyes tightly shut for a moment. Then, coolly, he set his eye once more to the scope. He couldn't see his target, but he knew the riders were coming fast. He drew a breath, let it half out, and squeezed the trigger, aiming at thin air.

The rifle stabbed a booming lance of flame. The barrel kicked high. Stark dropped flat and rolled out from behind the boulder. On his belly, he peered through the scope again. He was barely in time to see the two remaining horsemen race past the suddenly riderless and spooked horse of his target. The rider had just hit the ground. He must've run square into the path of the dropping bullet.

The other two horsemen jerked their mounts about. Stark could imagine their shock. To see their pard swatted from his saddle as if by a giant unseen hand, and maybe not even to have heard the shot that did it, was the stuff of nightmares for men who rode the outlaw trail.

The riderless horse settled down. It trotted a little distance, then stopped. The two men held a quick confab, likely trying to figure out what had transpired. They reached a quick decision. Wheeling their mounts, they set the spurs to them and bolted. They weren't returning to the pack out on the prairie. They were hitting the trail, clearly not willing to suffer the fate they'd just seen befall their comrade. In seconds, they were beyond the range of the scope.

A good shot, Stark thought with a bleak satisfaction. Three enemies disposed of for the price of one.

He wriggled backward, came to his feet, and, moving in a crouch, returned to his original cover at the rim of the plateau's face.

The cover fire from below had slackened off. No doubt some of the riffraff had seen the distant fall of one of their number, and the desertion of two more. No one set out to check on the fallen man, but after a moment the firing picked up again.

Stark frowned. What was their strategy now? They'd already seen that the effort to encircle him had failed. What else were they trying to cover up?

Still frowning, he used his field glasses on the grassland below. There was a only a slight breeze rippling the deep grass, and no cover to speak of between the face of his sanctuary and the stubborn rabble out on the plain.

In his mind Stark laid out a grid on that suspect open area, and then began a methodical examination of each sector of it. A faint movement of the grass made him pause. He waited, keeping his glasses trained on the spot, eyes unblinking. There. It came again. The tips of several blades of knee-deep grass swayed. Their movement was contrary to the direction of the wind. Stark nodded to himself.

Someone was crawling through the grass, either to get close enough for a shot, or to try to reach the base and scale the mesa unseen. Whoever it was down there was pretty good at stalking, Stark conceded. Was it the wolfer, who once more seemed to have vanished?

Keeping his eye on the telltale movement of the grass, Stark swapped the glasses for the Sporting Rifle and drew a bead down the long octagonal barrel. After his earlier shooting, this was tenderfoot stuff.

Putting a scare into the skulker would probably do as much good as trying to kill him. Rapid-fire, he drove two shots less than a foot in front of the unseen stalker.

Grass and clods flew. Stark writhed sideways. He didn't need glasses or scope to see the startled figure explode up out of the grass, arms flailing. A saddle gun went flying from his panicked grip.

Stark felt a twinge of disappointment. It wasn't the wolfer. Still, he grinned as he watched the jasper, rifle forgotten, go pelting back toward his comrades. Stark sent a bullet past his bobbing head to see if he could get a little more speed out of the fellow. He could.

Stark withdrew slightly to a different vantage point. With the ignominious retreat of their stalker, the gunfire from the rabble tapered off.

Stark swigged thoughtfully from his canteen. Their numbers had been thinned some, their assaults repulsed, but they didn't seem inclined to give up just yet. He figured he could start picking them off until they high-tailed it for good, but he'd already determined not to kill any more of them than need be. And there were still too many to try to outrun. So, he reckoned, he was back to waiting for nightfall.

He reconnoitered his stronghold once more and watered Red again. The stallion appeared content to crop the sparse grass and work it laboriously past the steel bit in his mouth. Leaving him to his grazing, Stark sought out the shade of a stone pillar. Leaning against it, he kept watch on his besiegers.

This delay irked him, but there was nothing for it but to wait while the sun slid lower in the sky. He gnawed a piece of jerky to still the distant grumble in his belly.

His thoughts turned to Gundance, who was surely the most dangerous of all those who might be looking to lift his scalp. How would the master bounty hunter play this game out? he pondered. How would a hunter like Trowbridge set out to catch his prey, when that prey was just as dangerous as the hunter himself?

Stark mulled it over. No sign of Trowbridge yet, but he was better at his job than any of the scoundrels who so far had tried to lay claim to his hide. And when it came time for the final hand to be dealt, Gundance would want it straight-up between them, hunter and hunted. He always gave his prey a chance to turn the tables on the hunter.

Then, slowly, Stark's mouth tugged upward in a grudging grin, because he knew just how Gundance would play this. It was exactly how he himself would've played it had he been on the hunt for Trowbridge. There was no more need to be looking over his shoulder for Gundance. The bounty hunter would show soon enough.

Just the same, Stark did glance over his shoulder. He hadn't forgotten the wolfer and his Big Fifty buffalo gun.

For a mite of a heartbeat he thought he was imagining things, seeing a mirage cast by the glaring sun overhead. Then the reflexes of a hunted beast lashed his muscles into action.

He twisted about and flung himself flat, levering the Sporting Rifle even as he moved. His finger convulsed on the trigger while he was still in midair. As it did, a solid piece of lead tore past his skull with a concussion of air that almost stunned him. He hit the ground flat on his chest, his eyes catching a blurred glimpse of the wolfer, not more than twenty feet away. The heavy Sharps he had just fired had been torn from his grip by Stark's instinctive snapped shot.

Before he could recover, or lever the rifle for a second shot, the wolfer came springing at him, the twelve-inch blade of a double-edged knife jutting from his fist. Stark reared to meet him, trying to line the rifle on the hurtling form. Still addled by the near miss from the huge buffalo gun, he was too slow.

The wolfer got past the barrel, batting it aside so that the weapon was knocked from Stark's grip. Then the wolfer was atop him, bearing him down, blade driving at his throat, yellowed teeth snapping in the furred muzzle of his face. The stench of wolf burned Stark's nostrils.

Stark twisted his head. He felt the coolness of the flat of the blade against the side of his neck as it drove by him to bury itself in the ground. Then he rammed the heel of his palm up against the wolfer's jaw, and used his whole body to heave the other man rolling sideward off of him. His head was clearing now; his body had reacted automatically.

He came up on his feet with the big bowie knife in his fist, its blade almost as long, and even broader, than that of the Arkansas toothpick wielded by his foe. His

.45 had been lost in the brief, fierce scuffle, and he knew he wouldn't be able to get the Marlin free in time.

So it was to be cold steel between them.

The wolfer appeared to savor the prospect. He flashed a feral grin that seemed to match that of the lupine skull at his waist. "Finally ran you to ground, ain't I?" he said in a guttural growl.

"That's the easy part," Stark said.

He was eyeing the other man's knife. Like the bowie, it was meant more for fighting than for anything else. Its blade was straight and double-edged, with a cross-guard to protect the user's hand. Stark's blade had a clipped point and a false edge, with a strip of brass welded along the top. Stark saw the flicker of the wolfer's eyes and knew he had recognized the brass strip as a trap to catch and hold the cutting edge of an opposing blade. The wolfer knew his way around knives.

"Shot my Big Fifty plumb out of my hands," came the growl. "Likely ruined it. You'll pay for that."

"Come on and collect," Stark invited.

And the wolfer accepted the invitation. He glided forward, left hand out to guard, right hand holding the knife in closer to his side. Stark's stance might've been a reflection. The wolfer made a feint with his left as if trying for Stark's knife wrist. On the heels of it, he lunged, straight and fast. The gleaming point of the Arkansas toothpick lanced for Stark's ribs. The wolfer was too smart to risk leaving himself open by a slashing attack this early in the game.

Stark snapped his bowie over to parry that darting lunge. The two big blades clashed together, then Stark drove in a thrust of his own. But the wolfer was just as quick, just as deft, with his own parry. Again the blades chimed, and the wolfer made his counter lunge.

For a searing passage of seconds it went on like that: a blurred, close-range exchange of steel. Time and again points were turned away inches from flesh. Neither man gave way. If the timing of either of them was off by a moment, or if the reflexes of either slipped at all, then the duel would've been over then and there.

In the midst of that savage interplay, Stark fancied an itching between his shoulder blades. If he was driven back too close to the rim, he might be the target for a lucky shot from one of the pack on the plain below. He made the next thrust high, aiming for the face. The wolfer flinched, and, step by step, stabbing and deflecting in turn, Stark drove him back from the edge.

The wolfer snarled and growled. His blade was his fang, and he was as savage as the big carnivores he hunted in its use. Unexpectedly he gathered himself and sprang a full yard backward so Stark's incoming thrust fell short. Instantly the wolfer sprang again, forward this time and to the outside. Pivoting on one moccasined foot, he came in from Stark's left.

Stark twisted away from the driving blade. He pivoted himself, sweeping the bowie around in a flashing arc at the wolfer's neck. The edge of the bowie scalped the fur hat from his head as he ducked. Again he sprang back to avoid Stark's return cut.

They circled like two lobos, panting from the intensity and effort of their exchanges. The wolfer was a wily fighter. He kept his blade moving, his torso shifting from side to side. Once he bobbed his head as a man might who was planning a low, lunging attack. It was a subtle feint, meant to lure in an opponent who relied on his foe's instinctive, unconscious movements to tele-graph his moves. Stark wasn't lured. He watched all of the wolfer, not concentrating on any particular part of him. Abruptly, he jerked his hand up to fake a throw. The wolfer only sneered. Neither of them was likely to fall for the other's feints.

The wolfer's next move wasn't a fake or a lure. He didn't telegraph it either. He dived into a tight, somer-saulting roll past Stark, slashing at his legs as he went by, trying for a hamstringing cut. Stark sidestepped. He glimpsed the arc of the wolfer's blade passing inches in front of his withdrawn leg. Before he could mount a counterattack, the wolfer had bounced back to his feet like a sideshow acrobat.

This boy was full of tricks. Stark came in jabbing with his bowie like a prizefighter in the ring. Head shift-ing like a snake's, the wolfer gave way. With no warn-ing he sank to one knee and shot his knife arm out straight. Stark almost impaled himself on that waiting blade. Gut sucked tight, he had to spin outside the un-orthodox thrust. He hewed down with the bowie at the wolfer's crouching form, but the lean killer tucked his head, rolled forward over his own shoulder, and bounded once more to his feet.

Back and forth they danced then to the harsh music of their blades. The guards of their fighting knives clashed together. They came face-to-face with the weap-ons locked between them. In the gasping, straining space of a heartbeat, Stark stared into feral, savage eyes inches from his own. They flung each another reeling apart.

At some point Stark had taken a cut on his left arm. Not serious, but it bothered him that he couldn't remember when it happened. He wouldn't remember the thrust that slid between his ribs either. . . .

The wolfer hawked and spat. His buckskins gaped from a cut on his side. Stark wondered if the wolfer recalled the thrust that had done it.

"Come on," the wolfer said suddenly, gritting. "Let's finish this! No more tricks. Straight in, and the toughest man walks away!"

"Yeah," Stark said coldly. "Straight in."

It might well be mutual suicide, a distant part of his brain warned him, but he charged to meet the wolfer's rush just the same. Then, as they came together, blades driving for flesh, the wolfer pulled a final trick. In midthrust he flipped the toothpick from right hand to left. Just as quick, just as sure left-handed as right-, he struck for Stark's heart.

Quicker, not fooled by the switch, Stark rotated his wrist so the keen blade of the bowie bit deep into the wolfer's outthrust left arm before the toothpick could find his flesh. Twisting the bowie free, he thrust over the wolfer's wounded arm, and felt his blade sink home.

The wolfer took a startled step back. Already his legs were sagging. He snapped at Stark one last time, then fell in a sprawl.

Stark stood over him, pulling in air hard. His tone was ironic. "No more tricks," he said.

On impulse, he stooped and slashed again with the bowie. It severed the soiled rope at the wolfer's gaunt waist. Stark kicked the skull totem away.

He understood that, while he'd been distracted by the

flankers and the creeper down on the plain, the wolfer had managed to get behind him after all. Scaling the rear of the butte, he'd slipped past Red and come deuced close to collecting the bounty. The angle of his approach must've kept him from firing sooner than he had.

Tired, Stark wiped the bowie clean in the grass. He found his Colt and slid it back in the holster. Then he collected the ruined Sharps and the wicked Arkansas knife.

He risked skylining himself with both weapons raised overhead. He stood there like some ancient statue of battle until he was sure he'd been spotted by the watchers out on the prairie. Then, deliberately, one after the other, he flung rifle and knife sailing far out from the crest of the butte.

After a moment a braver member of the pack put his horse forward at a wary lope. When he came to the two weapons, he sat his horse, staring down at the items. His shoulders sagged.

He took a last cheated look up at Stark's solitary figure, now holding the Sporting Rifle. Shaking his head, he wheeled his horse and galloped back to his waiting comrades.

Stark figured the message was clear enough. Their pack leader was dead. Without him, the curs couldn't hope to bring down the prey.

There were a few moments of palavering, some milling about, and then the bunch of them rode wearily away, leaving their dead behind them.

Stark waited until he could no longer discern their mounted forms even with the field glasses. They'd given up the hunt.

Stark glanced at the sun. Red had had time to rest. They could still make some distance before sunset.

Lucius Kincaid, and Gundance, would be waiting for him.

Chapter Ten

"We'll camp here," Heck Thomas declared, reining up in the shelter of a high, grassy ridge.

Prudence drew an inward sigh of relief. Despite her boasting to Evett Nix, now, after two days of hard riding, her seat had yet to grow accustomed to the saddle. As she dismounted from her palomino mare, she had to resist the quite unladylike impulse to rub that portion of her anatomy.

"Pitch Miss Prudence's tent over yonder," Heck directed. "We'll take turns standing guard again."

Before she set to helping with the chores, Prudence did allow herself to be so undecorous as to slap some of the dust out of her clothing. She wore a light tan riding outfit consisting of a divided skirt and matching jacket over a frilled white blouse. A petite flat-brimmed Stetson was perched on her head. She'd braided up her hair to keep it out of her way. A little .32-caliber revolver rode her trim waist on a narrow gun belt.

She knew from the covert looks Stand Garner had given her that she must make a fetching picture. She found herself hoping the rigors of travel didn't wear all the blush off that picture, then quickly quashed such frivolous thoughts.

For the most part the taciturn lawmen composing the

posse had treated her with a brotherly respect, which she appreciated. Garner had been boyish and charming, but had made no improper advances. Despite herself, she still found the big young deputy very attractive. Her anger at James Stark and his rash actions that had caused so much trouble still simmered at a low boil.

She had appointed herself camp cook, since she knew the lawmen, however gracefully they accepted it, saw her presence as a burden to them. Doing the cooking was one way she could earn her keep on the trail.

By the time dusk merged with darkness she had whipped up a supper of ham, biscuits, beans, and coffee. The lawmen chowed down with gusto, and she found herself flattered by their obviously sincere compliments.

"By Godfrey, if this ain't the best chuck I've ever enjoyed on the trail," Murphy, the most garrulous of the group, said when he'd finished his sizable helping.

Unreasonably pleased, Prudence set about cleaning up after the meal. The men wandered off a little ways to keep from interfering with her labor. Snatches of their conversation drifted to her as she labored. She heard Murphy's voice and paused involuntarily in her chores at his words.

"They say Gundance is on Stark's trail. That blamed bounty-hunting man-killer ain't no better than most of them no-luck hombres he brings in over the saddle, if you would ask me. Wouldn't mind having an excuse to drop a loop on him and haul him in to the hoosegow."

"Don't want to go up against him face-to-face, do you, Murphy?" one of the others joshed.

"Not hardly, Murphy snorted. "Don't rekcon there's

anybody who could face him and walk away afterward.''

Prudence blinked furiously several times and closed her ears to the rest of the talk. She bent over the skillet she'd been scraping.

"Don't pay no nevermind to them," the soft voice counseled. "That's just trail talk."

Startled, she looked up at the tall figure looming against the night. She hadn't heard Heck Thomas approach.

She rose, grateful for his comforting presence. "I'm worried about Jim." The words were hard to force past her lingering resentment. It was as though they were some kind of confession.

"I've ridden the trail with Stark," Heck advised. "He can fend for himself against just about anything that comes down the pike."

"Even against Gundance?" The question came before she could stop it.

Heck gazed up at the night sky. "Sometimes what's most important isn't which man can draw the fastest or shoot the straightest, but which man has the most to live for. Jim Stark strikes me as a man who has plenty to live for. All Trowbridge lives for is death."

Leaving her with his comments, he turned and moved away as silently as he had approached. What had he meant? she wondered, and didn't dare search her heart for the answer.

Finished with the cleanup, she stacked the tin plates so they'd be handy in the morning. She checked to be sure the coffeepot over the dying fire wasn't empty, then strolled past the gossiping deputies toward her tent. At some point the night air had taken a faint chill, and she hugged herself tightly.

Her action inevitably brought to mind the shameless way she had flung herself against Jim Stark in the hallway of her hotel the night before he'd ridden out on his vendetta. Blood rushed to her face at the memory, whether from embarrassment, or a secret pleasure at how good it had felt to hold him, even briefly, she wasn't sure.

What could've possessed her to behave in such a fashion? And the words she had uttered to him! How could she have told him to *come home* to her? She could only hope he hadn't understood those words which, during that moment of high emotions, had escaped from her lips. Surely they couldn't betray some deep, secret longing that she continued to deny. Could they?

And what had he done in response to her impulsive gesture? Left the hotel, then ridden out the next morning without so much as a by-your-leave, that's what! Now there was no question what brought the heat rushing to her face. The nerve of the man! She resisted the childish impulse to stamp her foot.

Of a sudden she regretted all the effort she'd gone to in trying to keep him out of trouble. It was his own violent lifestyle and his headstrong character that created his present problems. She'd be a fool to entertain even remote fantasies about life with such an insufferable man.

"Pretty evening, isn't it?" a masculine voice asked quietly.

Prudence jumped and wheeled like a cat when the rocking chair came down on its tail.

"I'm mighty sorry, Miss. I sure didn't mean to frighten you."

She let her breath out and managed to regain her composure. "Why, Deputy Garner, I didn't hear you approach." Her voice was still shakier than she would've liked. "What are you doing here?"

"Call me Stand. I'm taking the first round of guard duty, and just wanted to pay my respects. Like I was saying, I didn't intend to sneak up on you like that."

There was no doubting the genuineness of his contrition. For all his size, he moved as quietly as Heck Thomas. His nearness, the sheer masculine presence of him, was disconcerting, but not altogether unpleasant, she realized. "There's no harm done," she was able to say in level tones.

He gave a relieved grin. "I'm real glad to hear that. Miss McKay—may I call you Prudence?"

"Why, I suppose," she said automatically. Inexplicably she was reacting to him the same way she had when they'd met. During the two days on the trail, she had almost unconsciously avoided being near him. But now, looking past his broad shoulder, she saw that the other deputies at the fire seemed very far away indeed.

Emboldened by the liberty she'd granted, he relaxed some. "Mighty pretty evening, isn't it?" he repeated.

Involuntarily she turned her head to follow his gaze. The stars, not yet shining with their full brightness, had a fuzzy nimbus about them, making them glow almost warmly against the cold depths of blackness beyond. As she watched, a sudden golden streak etched itself across the sky, then faded, leaving its image flickering in her vision. She gasped aloud at the suddenness and beauty of it.

"A shooting star," he exclaimed softly. "Make a wish on it."

She turned her head back toward him and realized he had moved closer to her. Too close. She twirled about and put her back to him. But it would be rude to do more than that.

"You make a wish, instead," she said to cover her growing confusion. Glancing covertly over her shoulder, she saw him lift his face thoughtfully to the sky. There was a heady man scent to him, not unpleasant. Very little about this man was unpleasant.

"Well?" she prodded after a moment.

"What?" He sounded puzzled.

"Tell me your wish."

He hesitated, as if giving thorough consideration to her request. "That'll keep it from coming true," he protested.

She waited, keeping her back to him. She wondered why she was putting him to this silly test. She had to fight the urge to shiver.

He sighed in consent. "I reckon I wished for a home, a pretty wife, and some young 'uns. Maybe a business of some sort to run. A man can't spend all his days chasing outlaws."

Some men could, she thought with an edge of bitterness. "That's a nice wish." Her voice sounded a trifle hoarse in her own ears.

"Now you make one."

She shook her head. "There's only one wish per star. This one belonged to you."

She knew he had moved yet closer to her. If he lifted his big hands, they would settle quite naturally on her shoulders. She almost wanted them to.

What was happening to her? some remote part of her mind questioned frantically. Only moments before, she had been consumed with memories and secret longings for Jim Stark. It was foolish to be flirting with this relative stranger, appealing though he might be.

But why was it foolish? a more insistent voice demanded. There could never be anything of substance between her and Stark. Neither of them wanted it. In one way or another each had made that very clear.

Over her personal protests and appeals Stark had gone haring off to probably get himself killed. And even if he returned from this savage quest, it would only be a matter of time before he went traipsing off on some other bloody mission. To even think of linking her life to such a man was the most absurd of notions, contrary to the logic and reason by which she attempted to live.

Of course, that same logic argued that her law practice would hardly lend itself to the kind of woman Stand Garner wished for. Maybe she wasn't suited for any man.

Her heart was thundering, her head whirling. She sensed with a longing dread that he had lifted his hands. In a moment they would descend on her shoulders. Would he simply rest them there? Or would he turn her, irresistibly, into his embrace?

With every fragment of resolve she possessed, Prudence forced herself to step clear and then turn to face him. He was just lowering his big hands self-consciously to his sides.

"Good night, Deputy," she said in level tones that surprised her. "I hope you get your wish one day."

"I'm sure I will," he said confidently. "But it helps a wish to come true if two people wish for the same thing."

"I'm sure it does."

He hesitated. "I just need to know one thing."

"What is that, Deputy?"

"Call me Stand. And what I need to know is, are you spoken for?"

She almost blurted out, yes, she was. But that would be a lie.

Wouldn't it?

"No," she said, "I'm not."

"I'm mighty glad to hear that, Prudence. Good night."

He turned away, and Prudence fled thankfully to the sanctuary of her tent.

The following morning, she was reluctant to face him, but he only offered her a friendly grin and treated her with meticulous courtesy. She was relieved, but still watchful. She knew both he and Jim had figured somehow in her dreams last night. For her own modesty and peace of mind, she supposed it was just as well she didn't remember the content of those dreams.

Heck Thomas set the same determined pace he had maintained for the past two days on the trail. The lawmen rode like centaurs, with no fear evident, in this bastion of outlaws. Their arrogance was not without reason, Prudence knew. Even the roughest gang of desperadoes would think twice before tangling with a crew of deputies headed by Heck Thomas. When working for

Judge Isaac Parker, the Hanging Judge, Thomas had led a posse that brought in no less than thirty-two wanted men at once, following a sweep of these same regions. The feat was near legendary.

The day was pleasant, and patches of spring wild-flowers—yellow and violet and pink—lent rippling sprays of color to the windblown grass. If not for the mission that had brought her here, Prudence could've thoroughly enjoyed this outing.

Stand Garner spurred up beside her in high good humor. He made no reference to whatever had—or hadn't—occurred between them last night, but tried some sincere efforts at easy conversation.

Prudence kept her responses noncommittal. She was out here for a reason, she'd decided. And this was neither the time nor the place for romantic entanglements, even if she was interested in such. Perhaps, when all this was over, if Stand . . . Resolutely she set such speculations aside.

After a spell the young deputy dropped back, wearing a perplexed look on his handsome features.

Shortly following their brief noontime halt, a single rider hove into view on a nearby hill. After a moment's intense scrutiny of their party, he spun his mount and disappeared.

"Stand, Murphy, go fetch that fellow back here." Heck tossed the order over his shoulder.

The chosen pair streaked off in pursuit. They reappeared shortly, herding the solitary rider ahead of them like a maverick steer. Heck spurred out to meet them. A quick confab ensued.

Prudence realized the senior deputy intended to interrogate the stranger out of her earshot, doubtless due to some misplaced desire to protect her from unwelcome news.

She broke away from the other lawmen and pushed her mare to join the group. Heck glanced about with a scowl as she drew up, but she paid him no heed, listening instead to the rider's account.

He was a disheveled and disreputable-looking fellow. "We had Stark holed up on top of this mesa," he was reporting, plainly eager to please his interrogators. "Could've killed us all, I reckon, with that blamed buffalo repeater of his. But as long as we didn't press him none, he just held us off. Shot my hat plumb from my head." He indicated a ragged, fist-sized hole in his bedraggled sombrero.

Prudence felt a surge of relief that almost made her slump in the saddle. Thankfully, Stark hadn't gone on a killing rampage as she had half feared that he would. Seemingly he'd used only the force necessary to do his job. Well, that was most always how he had handled violence in her experience, she reminded herself.

But what would occur when he finally encountered Lucius Kincaid? How many would die then? And would Stark himself be among them?

"Keep talking," Thomas said, prodding the saddle tramp.

"Wolf, the fellow who we was sort of following, and who got us together in the first place, snuck up there to get him while we gave him cover. Next thing we know, Stark throws Wolf's gun and knife down from up top the mesa. We figured he must've got Wolf, instead of Wolf getting him. That's when we knew we didn't have no chance. So we pulled out.'' He glanced back over his shoulder as he finished, as though fearful of seeing his erstwhile prey looming on his back trail.

''Whereabouts is this mesa?'' Thomas demanded.

Prudence listened to the reply with only half an ear. She was assessing what she had heard. Apparently Jim hadn't hesitated to kill when necessary, but he was still alive and heading irrevocably toward disaster unless they could intercept him in time.

''Scat!'' Thomas dismissed the saddle tramp.

When the posse moved out, Prudence was fully aware of Stand Garner's shrewd, admiring gaze on her.

Chapter Eleven

Watching his own eyes in the upright oval mirror, Lance Trowbridge made his draw. He was gratified to hear Nona's startled gasp from the other side of the room. He was even more gratified to note that there hadn't been a perceptible flicker in his eyes to telegraph the draw. No opponent would be able to anticipate his move by watching his eyes.

Not even James Stark.

"Your hand," Nona said in tones of awe. "It never seemed to move! The gun was just all of a sudden there!" She sat at the vanity, her brush forgotten in her grip. Loosened, her dark hair fell in waves to her shoulders.

Trowbridge grinned at himself. He practiced his draw religiously every day, but he'd never let Nona hang around when he did so. She could be deuce distracting.

But he had let her watch today for a purpose. Girls like her talked. When Kincaid sent her and the blond back to the bawdyhouse or saloon that had spawned them, she would repeat the story and likely embellish it. In doing so, she would only add to his reputation, build up the legend of the invincible Gundance. It never hurt to have an hombre shaking in his boots before you ever reached for your gun to bring him down.

"I've seen men killed in gunfights before," Nona was saying. "But I've never seen anything so fast. Is that how you pull your gun when . . . when you kill someone?"

"Yeah, except then I pull it faster," Trowbridge answered.

"How many men have you killed?" Her voice was hesitant.

Trowbridge had been awaiting the question. She was high-dollar stock, but underneath the fancy trappings, she was still just another saloon girl, and they all got around to that question eventually.

Kincaid had offered no objection when she'd taken up lodging with Trowbridge here in the spacious third-floor room he was occupying. As requested, his quarters boasted a sweeping view of the front of the homestead.

The Eastern millionaire seemed content with the attentions of the blond, whose name Trowbridge had never cared enough to learn. When Kincaid grew tired of the two women, he would send them both packing, and replace them with two more. Nona had confided that the two of them had been there several months, and she wasn't sure how much longer this easy life would last. She'd be sorry to see it end.

Trowbridge had shrugged. "Surely a charming young lady like yourself could gain such a place in his affections that he'd make you Mrs. Kincaid."

He'd been serious, but she had sniffed scornfully, much as when they'd first met. "A man like Lucius doesn't give his name to a horse he buys. He keeps it for a spell, and then sells it or trades it off when he's finished."

She had a point, Trowbridge acknowledged. And he reckoned he himself fell pretty much into that same category. Kincaid had bought him as a tool to exact vengeance for the death of his son. A kept gun, he mused wryly, and took to the phrase. A kept gun, but a mighty expensive one.

"Something wrong, hon?" Nona's voice intruded. He never had answered her question about the number of his victims. "You're not very talkative this morning."

"He's out there," Trowbridge said after a moment. "I can feel him."

"Who? Oh, you mean . . ." she broke off as though fearful of offending him.

He paid her no more heed. She knew why he was here, just like he knew why Kincaid had brought her and the blond here. That didn't bother him, and his own purposes didn't seem to give her much concern. They were a lot alike; both of them were predators.

And he sensed that his prey was nearby, maybe walking into the trap already. The instinctive tension of the hunter was riding him. Enough time had passed for Stark to run the gauntlet. The waiting was almost over. Within the near future, Stark would make his play for Lucius Kincaid.

Did Stark know that he, Trowbridge, was lying in wait for him? Stark would suspect as much, Trowbridge guessed. Once having been hunted, the prey always knew when it was being hunted again. And it could always sense the identity of the most dangerous hunter. Stark had been both hunter and hunted plenty of times, and he'd always survived. The tribulations he had faced in coming this far would've only served to hone his skills to a razor's edge.

Trowbridge clenched and unclenched his gun hand. It ached for the grip of a .45, not in a practice showdown in front of a mirror, but in a real face-off, which was the only true gauge of a gunman.

Nona said something else that he didn't bother to listen to. He needed to make his usual rounds of the homeplace and question the outriders coming in off the nightly patrols of the surrounding countryside. Odds were, they wouldn't have seen anything, even if the Peacemaker was breathing down their necks. But he had to make sure.

Voices drifted up from the front porch of the house. Trowbridge crossed to the window. Standing to one side, he pulled the curtain back far enough to peer out.

A sorry-looking hombre on a spavined horse had been escorted in by two of Kincaid's outriders. He was trying to give an account of himself to the surly Break. The ex-prizefighter stood at the head of the steps, arms crossed in front of his broad chest. Trowbridge couldn't make out the stranger's words.

Here might be a fount of useful news, Trowbridge thought hopefully. Turning on his heel, he strode to the door, plucked his hat from the peg, and left the room. The closing of the door cut off Nona's resigned farewell.

By the time he legged it down the stairs, Break was escorting the stranger to Kincaid's den. Trowbridge fell in with them. The newcomer was a runty hardcase, who was looking about him with a greedy gleam on his pockmarked face. His shifty eyes narrowed at Gundance's approach.

Clad in a brilliant blue silk dressing gown, Kincaid was on his feet in the center of his study. A cigar jutted from between his teeth, and a glass of some of his fine whiskey was in his hand. A bottle stood open on the bar in the corner. The blond was nowhere in sight.

Eyeing the man he figured would be paying him ten thousand dollars before too long, Trowbridge felt a smug superiority. The millionaire was no longer quite the same highfalutin despot he had been on their first meeting.

As the days had passed with the bounty uncollected, and the rumors of Stark's relentless passage through the Territory trickled in, Kincaid's bland face had grown a little more pale and a little more gaunt. Worry lines furrowed his high forehead, and his beard was a trifle ragged. He even seemed to have shed a few pounds of lard from his bulk. Watching the glass in his hand, Trowbridge noticed the whiskey was in constant motion. Kincaid was shaking.

He looked sharply at the bounty hunter, but didn't otherwise acknowledge his presence. Trowbridge moved to where he could see the hardcase clearly. The little man had an empty holster, he noted.

"Tell me," Kincaid ordered without preamble.

"Yeah, sure, Mr. Kincaid," the jasper stammered. "Like I was telling your boys, me and my two pards almost had the Peacemaker a couple days ago."

"Almost?" Kincaid snapped. "You didn't get him?" Trowbridge fancied the little eyes buried in the fat face shuttled briefly to him. He kept watching the crowbait hardcase.

"Well, it was like this, Mr. Kincaid," that worthy

stumbled on. "We spotted Stark from a distance and got on his trail, kind of waiting for our chance, so to speak." Now it was he who glanced nervously at Gundance.

"Keep talking," Kincaid hissed.

"We seen him ride into some hills, and closed in fast," the narrator continued. "We figured once he was in the brush and draws of them hills, we could sneak up and get the drop on on him."

He winced at Trowbridge's contemptuous snort.

"And?" Kincaid snapped vehemently.

"We was riding down a draw, keeping our eyes peeled, following his tracks, when all of a sudden this voice, cold as ice, says from behind us, 'If you boys are looking for me, then the hunt's over.' We turn around, and he's standing on the ridge of the draw above us, big as life, looking meaner than the devil himself." The hardcase paused to draw breath.

"We starts to make our plays, but he's throwed down on us with that blamed repeating shotgun he carries. All he does is lever it once, and we knowed we didn't have a hope, not bunched up down in that draw like we was." His face had gone a little pale at the memory.

"What'd he do?" Kincaid said too quickly.

"Told us to drop our guns and light a shuck out of there."

"He spotted you trailing him, led you into an ambush like you were sheep, disarmed you, and sent you packing," Gundance summarized coldly. "Lucky he didn't blow you to pieces just for the time you cost him."

The cigar between Kincaid's teeth moved jerkily. It had gone out at some point. Using his free hand, he fumbled with a soiled linen handkerchief and mopped at his forehead. "That's what happened? You ran out?"

"Didn't have no choice, what with him looming up there like Death himself. He must've moved quiet as a haint to Indian up on us like that." He shook his head at the image fixed in his mind.

"Why did you come here?" Kincaid asked sharply.

"Well, since we sort of put our necks on the line trying to collect that bounty, and since you're willing to pay five thousand dollars to have him dead, I figured it might be worth something to you to know where he was when we seen him."

"How long ago did this happen?" Trowbridge cut in.

"Day before yesterday, late in the afternoon."

"And you rode straight here?"

"Well, we holed up for the night. My pards didn't want nothing else to do with the Peacemaker, so I came on here alone."

"Then, since you're here, Stark could be here too," Trowbridge concluded. "Ain't that right?"

"I reckon so." The jasper looked as though he didn't like the notion.

Trowbridge turned a triumphant gaze on Kincaid.

"Well, what about it, Mr. Kincaid?" the saddle tramp whined. "What I'm telling you ought to be worth something—"

"Throw this trash out of here!" Kincaid barked.

In a trice Break had the hapless hombre headed through the door in a bum's rush. A howl of outrage was cut off abruptly by by the meaty sound of a blow from the hallway outside the room.

Kincaid's big body was heaving. He chawed down so

hard on his cigar that his teeth bit almost through it so it sagged over his pendulous chins. With a stifled curse he snatched it from his lips and hurled it to the floor.

He swung toward Kincaid with an angry, almost accusing glare. "Well?"

Trowbridge shrugged casually. "Nothing's changed. I told you all along he was headed this way. Just a matter of time, and the time's about up."

"That's it?" Kincaid sputtered. "We don't do anything?"

Trowbridge strolled over and claimed a cigar from the humidor on the bar. He thumb struck a wooden match to get it lit. "Do whatever you want," he answered as he puffed. "It won't make a lick of difference. He'll still get here, and I'll still be waiting."

"You're no help!" Kincaid stomped petulantly to the bar and splashed more whiskey into his half-empty glass. "What if he's out there with that blasted long-range rifle, waiting to pick me off?" he snarled over his shoulder.

"That's not his style. But if it makes you feel better, don't go outside, and stay away from any unshaded windows. And as for me being a help, when he gets here, I'll be all the help you need."

"You talk mighty big."

Trowbridge smiled happily around his cigar. "That's right," he agreed. "And when the time comes, I'll back it up."

Kincaid slugged down his drink and sloppily refilled the glass. His voice was slightly slurred. "Do you really think you can beat him?"

Trowbridge plucked the cigar jauntily from his

mouth. "I'm betting my life and ten thousand dollars on it." He was enjoying watching the fat man sweat.

"No!" Kincaid spat, "I'm betting *my* life and ten thousand dollars!"

"That bounty doesn't seem like such a good idea now, does it?" Trowbridge prodded deliberately.

"It's a good idea!" Kincaid countered vehemently. "Whatever it takes to see James Stark dead is a fine idea!"

"He'll take his time," Trowbridge mused aloud, eyeing the millionaire. "He'll know I'm waiting for him."

Kincaid blanched, to Trowbridge's immense satisfaction. "You think Stark is expecting you to be here?"

"He'll be pretty sure I'm here, seeing as how I haven't caught up with him yet."

Kincaid stared hard at him, his fleshy chins working. He squared his shoulders and struggled to regain some of his composure. "If you really think he's close, I'll bring in the outriders and tighten their patrols. I'll also double the guard on the house."

A little disappointed at the millionaire's recovery, Trowbridge hitched his shoulders carelessly. "Suit yourself."

Normally it wouldn't have mattered to him whether or not Stark managed to kill Kincaid. The bait for a trap was usually expendable. But in this case, if he lost the bait he'd also lose the ten-thousand-dollar bounty Kincaid would pay him for Stark's hide.

Grudgingly he said, "I'll stick close to you from now on. For Stark to get to you, he'll have to come through me."

Relief showed on Kincaid's face.

"And arm yourself with something in addition to that peanut hideout rig on your arm," Trowbridge added.

Kincaid nodded decisively. His moment of weakness was fully past. He was once more the shrewd, ruthless businessman. Suddenly he looked like a dangerous man to cross. "I've got a few tricks if I have to use them. And I'll have Break stay close by as well."

"One thing," Trowbridge advised.

"What's that?"

"When Stark gets here, don't either you or your bullyboy get in my way. Is that clear?"

"Just do your job when the time comes."

Trowbridge smiled unexpectedly. "I'm looking forward to it," he said honestly.

Already, he could almost hear the humming.

Chapter Twelve

Lucius Kincaid had built his fortress in a wide, shallow vale between banks of rolling grassy hills. The hills would serve to blunt the force of the twisters often spawned by spring and summer storms. Of course, Stark reflected darkly from his vantage point in those hills, Kincaid's stronghold looked plenty capable of withstanding a twister, or just about anything else that came down the trail.

Including him.

There was scant cover, and more than one pair of patrolling outriders had come mighty close to stumbling over him. He had waited tensely, ready to deal with them if need be. But disposing of a couple of outriders at this juncture wouldn't have gotten him any closer to their boss. In fact, he would've been only worse off, since his victims would be missed. And, despite his having made it this far, he was bad enough off now, without anything else being added to his burdens.

Miles behind him, he had left Red in a range of rugged, overgrown hills and donned his high-topped Apache moccasins in place of his riding boots. Then, on foot and under cover of darkness, he had set out for Kincaid's sanctuary, armed for grizzly.

Evading the outriders at night hadn't been hard. He'd

felt like a wraith slipping by their towering forms, or lying low until they passed. He was a little surprised at just how far Kincaid had spread his protective cordon.

Only occasionally did an eerie feeling of being watched brush him like the faint draft from the wings of a passing owl.

He'd had a little trouble actually finding the fortress, and daylight found him still short of it. Progress became slower then. But on two feet, on hands and knees, and sometimes on his belly, he managed once more to slip past the guards. Set a bunch of horsemen to patrol, and they'd spend most of their time looking for another rider, not a man who could travel through the tall grass like a varmint or a snake, and leave scarcely a ripple in his wake.

Finally, his knees and belly aching, he'd found a site overlooking the homestead, and snugged down to watch. Over him he'd pulled the thin mat of woven grass he'd been working on each night almost since he'd left Guthrie. His hunch that it might come in handy had paid off. Lying on his chest, with the mat spread completely over him like a blanket, he could pass at a distance as nothing more than an irregular bulge in the terrain, unnoticeable to the casual glance of an eye.

There was always the chance he might be spotted if a rider came too close, but there was an awful lot of grassland and hillside for even a small army of lookouts to cover every square foot. So far, he'd been blessed with good luck, and hadn't gotten more than a roving look from the riders who come near in their irregular circuits.

Hat off, field glasses in his hands, he lay as still as

the ground itself and peered from under the edge of the mat. The woven grass trapped and held the heat, so he was sodden with sweat that caked the dust and dirt on his clothes and body. Where the grass touched his skin it tickled and itched. He ignored the discomfort, studying the layout of Kincaid's stronghold.

There were several outbuildings, including a sizable bunkhouse and a barn with an attached horse corral. A windmill turned rhythmically in the wind. He'd counted enough hired guns coming and going on patrol to be discouraging. A handful loafed around out front. He was going up against heavy odds. And they'd be even heavier if Gundance was, as he suspected, waiting for him inside. He supposed it was something of high praise that the bounty hunter figured he'd ever be able to even get into the house. He had his own doubts about being able to do it.

He saw no sign of Trowbridge, nor of anyone he took to be Kincaid. Drapes were drawn on most of the windows, although he did catch a glimpse of a blond woman who would've graced a high-dollar bordello. Kincaid didn't seem to be sweating his arrival very much, he thought sourly.

Come night, he'd circle the compound and take a look at the rear of the structure. He didn't expect to find any weaknesses. While he might set the outbuildings afire to stir things up, the stone house itself would be all but invulnerable to the flames.

Grimly he calculated what he would most likely have to attempt to have any chance of reaching his enemy. If he could silently dispatch a pair of the outriders, he could take the place of one of them, and, with the body of the other slung over a saddle, make a bold approach to the house, then try to bluff or shoot his way inside.

It was a two-bit sort of a plan, he thought darkly, but it still stood the best chance of success, so far as he could see. Brooding over it, he waited for night.

With full darkness, he folded his mat, slung both saddle guns on his back, and worked his way stealthily around toward the rear of the building, staying to the hills where possible.

As he crossed the valley floor, the sensation of watching eyes again raised the hackles on his neck. He paused, crouching, probing the night with his senses. He picked up nothing but the scents and noises of the night—sagebrush, the rustle of a field mouse. Could be, his nerves were stretched so taut he was just feeling them vibrate.

Not fully satisfied with that conclusion, he catfooted on across the flat. The lights of the house and outbuildings were a couple of hundred yards distant. There was no unusual activity there that he could detect.

He ascended swiftly into the hills on the far side of the valley, glad to be in their shelter. Once he went belly down on the ground as the silhouettes of two outriders moved past on the crest of a nearby ridge. They vanished in the darkness, and he ghosted on.

Finally he hunkered down in a shallow draw. Gazing over its rim, he could see the structures below. The shadow figures of mounted guards passed in front of the windows. Kincaid had taken plenty of precautions for his coming.

The hair at the nape of his neck sprang suddenly erect. He was swiveling to his feet, swiping his Colt from leather even before he fully realized that he'd somehow sensed the unseen watcher closing in from behind him.

"Now, just you don't go shooting me, white man," a quiet voice advised casually.

Stark sank to one knee, covering what he took to be a human figure framed against the night. "Show yourself," he ordered in a terse whisper. Whoever this was, he understood with a chill, had all but climbed into his hip pocket without being detected.

"No need to get jumpy," the quiet voice counseled. "Don't want to let them know we're here. I'm showing myself right now."

The vague form took substance as a slight figure with upraised arms. There was no gleam of a face, and Stark realized that the stranger was a black man. An old black man in shabby clothes, he added mentally as he got a better look in the dim light. The oldster didn't seem to be armed. And if he'd wanted to betray Stark's presence, he could've easily done it before now.

"Get down here!" Stark commanded. "Stay low!"

"Reckon I been doing that more years than you've been alive." The easygoing voice bore an edge of wry humor. "But I got to admit, you're pretty good at it yourself." There was a hoarseness to his tones, as though he might not have much occasion to speak out loud.

He knelt agilely, with no creaking of joints, some five feet distant from Stark, who saw the nod of his head beneath his sagging hat. "No need for that hogleg," the old man said. "I ain't looking to do you no harm. Might even be of some help."

"We'll see. Who are you?" This was a foolish place to be holding a confab, but unless he wanted to drill the mysterious old codger, Stark didn't see how he had much choice.

"Name's Silas. That's all, just Silas," came the whispered reply to his query.

"What are you doing here?"

"Live here."

Stark stared at the vague hunched form. "You mean down there with Kincaid?"

"Naw, I mean in these hills, the prairie, wherever I please. Been here a lot longer that Mr. High and Mighty Kincaid. That man done forgot that us slaves were freed a long spell back."

Stark didn't try to probe the mysteries the words raised. "Why have you been following me?" he asked instead.

"Mostly trying to see what you're up to. If it's what I think, then, like I said, I might be able to give you a hand."

"And just what is it you think?"

The old man calling himself Silas took a moment to answer. "Like me," he said then, "I figure you got some kind of grudge against the lord and master down in that fancy rock house. You been prowling around trying to figure out a way to pry him out, or to get inside. Ain't that right?"

Stark made a sudden decision. Whatever Silas's motives, they were pushing their luck in staying here. He motioned with the Colt. "Move out."

"Where we headed?"

"Hopefully someplace we can palaver without having Kincaid's guards stumble over us. Got any ideas?"

"Yep, as it happens, I do." Silas rose to a crouch. Once again he did it with the ease of a much younger man. "Follow along. And don't get jumpy. First, I got to collect my rifle."

"Just keep it pointed away from me."

Silas muttered something about sorry, mistrusting ingrates, and moved off, staying low to the ground. Stark followed. He almost lost track of the old man in the first few yards, so silently did he glide along. A hermit, or some such, Stark speculated, living out here for reasons maybe good only to him.

Hardly pausing, Silas scooped up his long gun. He made no effort to turn it on Stark, but slipped silently through the darkness, almost as if he'd forgotten his companion's presence. For his part, Stark was hard put to keep up. Ruefully he holstered his Colt and concentrated on the elusive form flitting through the gloom ahead of him.

When Silas came to an abrupt halt, Stark froze as well. His ears caught the creak of saddle leather and the snort of a horse. He ducked in the same heartbeat as did Silas. The pair of guards rode blindly past twenty feet in front of their prone forms. Clearly, avoiding such hazards was nothing new to Silas.

They went on. Stark knew he was being led farther and farther from his horse and from his prey. But Silas seemed to have a definite destination in mind. That notion was proven when he stopped in a flat span of grass in the shelter of one of the last hills in the range.

Stark could see nothing to distinguish this spot from

any other, but Silas bent and fumbled in the deep buffalo grass. With a grunt of effort he straightened, lifting what looked to be a four-foot-square section of the ground itself. With another snort of effort he shifted it aside, revealing the black mouth of a hole in the ground.

Stark realized the section of the prairie Silas had removed was really a concealed trapdoor of sorts, a kind of camouflaged plug for the mouth of the ominous hole.

Without further preliminaries Silas hopped down into the darkness. The cavity was deep enough so the top of his head was beneath the edge. Stark saw the flash of the whites of his eyes as he looked up expectantly for him to follow.

Poised at the edge of the hole, Stark hesitated. Hanged if he'd jump down there into pitch darkness.

"Come on," Silas ordered gruffly. "Ain't nothing but a hole in the ground. Lots more comfortable than a grave. I sure ain't fool enough to strike no light for you to see by, not with half an army of gun-happy yahoos looking for us. Nothing down here's going to hurt you none."

Mastering his reservations, Stark dropped down into the cavity, hand on his Colt. He ducked as Silas wrestled the heavy plug back into place. Stark understood that chunks of sod must've been placed atop the wooden lid and allowed to grow, making the trapdoor all but invisible to even a close inspection. A searcher could literally ride right over their heads and never be aware of them.

He was plunged into complete and total darkness as the lid settled back into place, leaving him at Silas's mercy. But then, he conceded wryly, that had pretty much been the state of affairs since the first moment he'd encountered the old black man. Just the same, he kept his hand on the butt of the .45.

He heard Silas fumbling a bit in the darkness. There was the clatter of glass on metal, the smell of coal oil, and then a match flame flared like an explosion. Involuntarily, Stark winced. He saw Silas applying the flickering flame to the wick of a battered lantern.

"Don't usually have no need for this," the old man was muttering. "Not much down here to see, and I already know where everything is."

As his eyes adjusted, Stark saw his host had been right. They were in a mostly barren dirt-walled cell about seven feet square. There was a pile of what he guessed was bedding, a small stash of tinned food, a couple of gunnysacks with unguessable contents, and a jug. Not a stick of furniture was in evidence. The ceiling was low enough so he couldn't stand erect, although Silas could manage it with a few inches to spare.

In the uncertain light of the lantern, Stark got his first look at his companion. Silas was small and wiry. His hands were the biggest thing about him. They were large and knobby, and looked hard as rocks. Deep creases and wrinkles in his weathered face made a shadowy spiderweb pattern across his features. He'd tossed his disreputable slouch hat aside, revealing a mat of curly hair shot through with paths of gray that shone almost white in the lantern's flame.

The saddle gun he'd been toting was leaning in a corner. It was an old lever-action of indeterminate make. Aside from a small skinning knife, he didn't seem to be armed. His clothes were a ragged collection of patched castoffs and furs.

"You live here?" Stark queried bluntly.

"Naw, this is just one of my gopher holes. I got a few of them scattered around. They come in mighty handy sometimes for laying low or riding out a norther." He gestured at the dirt floor. "Quit pawing your gun and sit down. You look powerful uncomfortable all hunched over thataway."

Suiting action to his words, he sank down himself into a cross-legged position, like a spring coiling. Stark shrugged off his shotgun and rifle and followed suit. He wasn't sure he did it quite as smoothly as Silas.

They ended up sitting almost knee to knee. Stark could smell the sweat and dirt on himself, the musky scent of his companion, and the dusty odor of the stuffy subterranean chamber.

"What's your beef with Master Kincaid?" Silas demanded. He made the title a thing of scorn.

Tersely, Stark explained, keeping his voice low, as did his host.

Silas snorted when he finished. "So, what are you fixing to do?"

"Get him to cancel the bounty," Stark told him.

"How you figure to do that?"

"Kill him, if I have to."

"Guess that'd cancel it, sure enough." The lined planes of Silas's face seemed constantly to merge with the darkness and then re-form. "You was watching the fortress trying to figure out how to get to him, weren't you?"

"Yeah," Stark confirmed.

"All these extra riders here to guard against you?"

"I figure so."

Silas gave a half shake of his head. "You must be one ring-tailed bearcat for Kincaid to be that worried."

"Only when I'm riled," Stark said with a growl. "Can you help me get to Kincaid?"

"Why, I reckon I can take you right under them guards' noses, and walk you plumb into that fancy house," Silas answered with conviction.

Chapter Thirteen

"I spotted you coming in on foot," Silas explained, "and wondered whether you was the cause of all this ruckus lately. Been renegades and gun trash prowling all over these parts. Anyway, I followed you to see what you was up to. Didn't get too close; you're too consarned good. Move like a puma. Might've spotted me and killed me just out of reflex, I figured."

Stark recalled the eerie sensations of being watched as he traveled cross-country. Silas moved pretty much like a puma himself. "How'd you come to be out here?" he asked, puzzled and curious about his seeming ally.

Silas sighed. He reached behind him without looking and snagged the jug. Unstoppering it, he propped it on his bent arm and drank. "Springwater from back in the hills." He offered it. "Cuts the dust."

Stark accepted the jug, balanced it on his arm, and took a pull. The water was slightly cool from its storage. He sloshed it around in his mouth, then swallowed gratefully. He gave the jug back to Silas, who plugged it and returned it to its spot against the wall.

"Been out here for years," he recounted in belated answer to Stark's question. "Wandered out here after the War Between the States. I fought wearing the Yankee blue. Lots of boys died trying to see me and the other slaves set free. Shouldn't ought to be legal for one man to own another.'' Grim memories stirred behind his words. Stark listened silently.

''I'd had enough of fighting and people, both black and white,'' Silas continued. ''So, after the war, seeing as how I was free, I figured I could go and do as I chose. So I came out here to get away from folks.'' He paused thoughtfully. ''There sure enough weren't many folks out here then. There was the Indians, and I lived with some of them, one time or another. Learned a lot about how to get by. But they was still people, and eventually, I'd pack up and move on.

''Living was pretty easy, if you knowed how. Plenty of game. There were buffalo. By heaven, you should've seen the buffalo! Can't hardly believe they're all but gone now.'' He looked about in the surrounding gloom like he expected to find the ghosts of the vanished herds lurking there.

Thirty-odd years he'd lived out here in the fastness of the prairie, Stark reflected in awe.

''I hunted and trapped, bartered some when I had to with the wild Indians and the trading posts that started springing up. Always did my best to avoid fighting. Like I said, had me enough of that in the War. Things were good, but the railroads came, and so did the buffalo hunters, and the prairie started getting smaller and smaller. Felt like I was being hemmed in, trapped.'' He cocked a shrewd eye at Stark. ''Reckon as how you've felt that way your own self sometimes, if I'm right at reading the breed of man you are.''

He was reading him right enough, Stark acknowledged silently. "I savvy," he said aloud.

"Eventually they started shipping the defeated tribes here; pretty much penned them up. Mighty big pen, but a pen just the same, the way I look at it."

Stark savvied that too.

"The renegades began flocking here next, like civilization was closing in on them. I hear a few things now and again. Guess the cities and the farms are coming closer and closer."

Stark nodded mutely. He wasn't sure Silas saw the movement.

"Black, white, red, don't matter the color of a man's skin if he's a renegade. Means he's turned on his own kind, like a rogue buffalo. Seems like the renegades are thick as fleas in these parts nowadays. Law and order must be on its way." He twitched his head sideward and spat on the dirt floor. "Ain't sure that's too much better sometimes."

"It's better," Stark avowed. "When it's in place, there's ways to deal with rogues like Kincaid." He wanted to rein the old man's talk back to the Eastern millionaire.

Silas didn't oblige him immediately. "I gather you make your way hunting renegades," he surmised. "But under the skin you ain't so much different from them sometimes."

"Blessed be the the Lord, who teaches my hands to war and my fingers to fight," Stark murmured.

Silas brightened. "The Good Book!" he spoke with pleased recognition. "That's what makes you different from the renegades."

148 *Clifford Blair*

"I hunt them," Stark conceded. "Right now, I'm hunting Lucius Kincaid."

"I figure he's about the worst of them," Silas said. "He maybe doesn't do much of the robbing and killing with his own hands all the time, but a lot of it gets done on account of him. I ought to know."

"How's that?" Stark prodded.

Silas kept quiet for a spell. Stark got the impression that he had never shared with another soul what he was about to impart.

"Got me a dugout over in the mountains," Silas said at last. "Reckon you could say that's where I live, though I don't spend much time there. Went up in them mountains after Kincaid came to these parts. I come back down to keep an eye on him. Like I said, I ain't one for fighting. I don't hold with killing, even when a man deserves to die. So I ain't never raised a hand against him, but I can't quite put what he done out of my mind."

"What was it?"

"A few years back, it came to me I wasn't getting no younger. Didn't feel much different, but sometimes my shooting eye wasn't what it once was when I went to hunt game. And I could see the gray starting to show in my hair when I drank from a stream or spring. Starting to look like an old silvertip girzzly. Dawned on me one day that I'd like to leave something of myself behind me when I'm gone. Guess that's only natural.

"I went and spent a spell with Indians I'd knowed. Kept my eye out, and finally settled on a sweet young gal who I thought would make a fine bride, and a mother for my son—I knew all along I'd have a son when the time came. And I could tell she looked with some favor on me, even though I was a heap older than her. Wouldn't have done nothing if I wasn't sure she'd have me.

"I went about it all proper and formal with her family, and she and I finally got hitched the Indian way. I had a circuit preacher, who visits the tribes, say the words for us as well, when we had the chance." His seamed face split in a wide grin. "There I was, married up and settled down, after all them years on my own."

Such marriages weren't uncommon, Stark knew. Many times they worked well. And Silas had gone about it in a civilized fashion. Stark didn't doubt that the old man would've made a loving and devoted husband for his bride.

"What was her name?"

Silas's grin turned to a fond smile. "Indian name translated to something like Spring Breeze. I always just called her Spring."

Stark didn't prod him any further. This account belonged to Silas. He could tell it in whatever fashion he pleased. Remotely, Stark wondered what he himself would leave behind him when he was gone.

"We didn't stay with her tribe. We came here to a place I'd picked out in the valley; built us a soddy. Cut the blocks of sod right out of the ground, and stacked them up good and solid. Added a roof. Made us a real sturdy house."

Built right, and maintained, such structures were surprisingly durable. They were better than a lot of the ramshackle shacks Stark had seen in towns. Farm families without access to lumber often resorted to soddies.

"And just like I knew she would, Spring done gave me a son!" Silas exclaimed. "Fine strapping lad, he was. Apple of my eye! Spring was a good mother to him, likely better than I was a pa. Looked a lot like her, he did—'course, in a manly way, you understand.

"I stayed as close to home as I could, what with seeing they was provided for proper. Her people helped us out, and we had us a good life. I took to wondering why I'd waited so long to start me a family. Figured I'd be good for two or three more young 'uns at least!"

His voice slowed unexpectedly, grew deep and brooding. "He had about five years on him, I'd guess. It was coming on winter, and I headed out to make one last round of my traps in the hills. After that, I swung by the trading post to swap for supplies so we could settle in for the winter. Was gone nigh onto a month."

Of a sudden he stopped speaking, as if his story was over. The shadows about his face seemed to darken. "When I got back, the soddy was gone," he resumed slowly. "Vanished like it'd never been there at all. A bunch of men was camped on the spot. One of them was Lucius Kincaid. With him he had a passel of hired guns, a couple of builders, and a pack of Mexicans and town Indians he'd hired as workers. They were fixing to build that big fancy house right smack-dab where my soddy had been standing when I left.

"Took me a spell to learn what happened. Seems Kincaid had picked this spot to build, just like me. Didn't matter none to him that my home was already there. Had his men tear it down. Turned Spring and my boy out with a norther blowing in. They didn't have no choice but to try to make it back to her tribe on foot.

Had nothing but the clothes on their backs. Turned out like dogs, they was!

"I found them with her people. They'd made it, but the trek was too much for them. The fever took them, took them both, not much more than a day apart. They was all but gone by the time I reached her people's camp. It was Kincaid that killed them, maybe not with his own hands, but it was him turned them out on the prairie in the teeth of that norther!"

"What did you do?"

Silas started to answer, then tensed. He held up a quick hand for silence. Stark heard or sensed it then. The faintest of vibrations could be felt from the ground above. He recognized the impact of hooves of approaching horses. A pair of the outriders were almost on top of the concealed pit.

Automatically Stark's hand stole to the butt of the .45. Silas, he noted, showed no real alarm, just an air of cautious waiting. He sat with his head cocked slightly, gazing up at the trapdoor.

The hoofbeats grew nearer. Like the pairs Stark had seen on patrol, these lookouts weren't in much of a hurry. He found himself gazing tensely up at the trapdoor as well. A small sifting of dust filtered down. Stark wrinkled his nose. It'd sure enough be a tenderfoot move for him to sneeze now. The outriders were actually riding over the sod-covered trapdoor.

Their hoofbeats passed on. Stark let himself relax. Silas lowered his gaze. His grief momentarily forgotten, he grinned a wicked conspiratorial grin. Stark gave a shake of his head in amazement at the old man's ability to exist literally under the feet of his enemies.

"They ain't never found me yet," Silas boasted as if in answer to his thoughts.

"You never went after Kincaid?"

Silas sobered. The shadows once more darkened his face. "I left Spring's people, decided I was better off all by my lonesome after all. But I couldn't forget what happened. I came back here, stayed in these hills, watched him build his big house. I never seen no slave driver work men harder than he worked those Mexicans and Indians he'd brought with him. Saw one try to escape once. Kincaid's men shot him down. After that, there weren't no complaints."

Silas paused and drew a deep breath of the stuffy air. "Sure enough, I could've killed Kincaid, was I of a mind to. Had me plenty of chances to use my rifle. Likely could've hid from his gunhounds and got clean away too. But I ain't no cold-blooded killer, not even of a man like Kincaid. I just don't have the gumption in me no more. But I can't quite bring myself to stay clear. I keep coming back, hoping I'll be around to see him get what's coming to him."

Silas had earlier dubbed himself a coward. Stark didn't share his opinion. He didn't think the old black man was afraid. Silas had been seared by the cruelty of slavery and branded by the violence of war. He'd kill if forced to, but not out of spite or vengeance.

"I'll give Kincaid what's coming to him," Stark said aloud. "He's got to be stopped. He's worse than the slaveholders in the old days. He thinks he's a law unto himself."

"Does whatever he thinks is right in his own eyes,

just like the Good Book says about the wicked," Silas agreed.

"Tell me how to get into that fortress. One way or another, I'll stop him."

"Reckon I can see my way clear to do that. Knew when I first seen you that you was after him, and that likely you'd need my help."

"How do I get in?" Stark had to force his teeth apart to speak.

"I'll have to show you."

"Show me what?"

Silas scratched at his curly hair. "Think on it. What does a varmint do when it digs a den?"

"Leaves itself a back way out," Stark said slowly. "But the rear of the house is just as secure as the front."

"Ain't talking about the backside of the house. Remember, I watched it being built, from the cellar up."

"A hidden passage." Stark breathed with dawning understanding. "Kincaid left himself some kind of secret escape route."

Silas was nodding. "For a fact, that's what he done. Mind you, I ain't never used it, but I seen it dug; I know where the outside exit is. Best I can figure, it leads back into the cellar. You'd still have to find him, once you was inside."

"I'll find him."

"I calculate we best wait till near morning. Might be hard to spot exactly where the exit is without a little bit of light. It's covered up some."

Stark didn't argue. The accumulated exertions and pressures of days spent on the run were beginning to weigh down on him like a load of lead. Silas curled up in a corner on the bedding. In moments his breathing became deep and regular.

Stark shifted about until his back was propped against the dirt wall, and dropped his chin onto his chest. Rifle under his hand, he slept as well.

Chapter Fourteen

Silas, stirring about, awoke Stark. The lantern flickered feebly in the underground cell.

"About time we moved out," the old man advised. "Here, swallow these down." He offered a tin of peaches.

Stark knuckled his eyes and accepted the meal gratefully. The syrupy fruit quenched his morning thirst and stilled the growling in his belly. Finished, he took stock. He was a bit sore from his unyielding bed, but overall he was feeling fit enough for the trail.

Silas listened for a spell, then reached up to grasp handholds on the bottom of the earthen plug. Stark helped him ease it aside. Cool, fresh air flowed in. After peering about in the early-morning gloom, they clambered out of the pit. Night still held its claim, but there was the beginning of a glow, off to the east.

Stark followed Silas, skulking through the hills and down into the valley holding Kincaid's abode. They crept on hands and knees, and sometimes on knees and elbows, through the heavy grass on the valley floor. Once, they flattened themselves, as outriders passed perilously close.

"Boss says to keep a sharp eye out," one of the riders commented.

''What in blazes does he think we been doing all this time?'' the other groused. ''I didn't hire out my gun to spend time sitting a saddle like some no-account cowpoke.''

His pard's reply was lost as they rode on. The yahoo might've made a better cowpoke than sentry, Stark reflected wryly. Silas was already up and moving like a prairie wolf stalking a rabbit.

Moments later the old man halted at one of the small rock outcroppings that thrust up occasionally from the grass. Crouching low, eyes fixed on the shadowed ground, he advanced slowly, sliding his feet rather than lifting them.

Stark swiveled his head this way and that. No more mounted guards were in evidence. The massive house was some hundred yards distant. The glow to the east was gradually pushing back the curtain of the night sky. Black was turning to deep violet at the curtain's edge, and the stars were fading. Much longer, and they'd be sitting targets for any sharp-eyed lookout gazing in their direction.

Silas came to an abrupt halt and grunted in satisfaction. He rubbed the toe of his moccasin back and forth on the ground in front of him. Stark moved up beside him. Silas's sliding foot had encountered the smooth surface of a small wooden trapdoor set flush with the prairie soil. Only a thin covering of accumulated dust and debris had served to conceal its presence.

Kneeling, Silas brushed at it with eager hands. Stark eyed the stone house. Details were becoming clearer to his naked eye.

Silas scrabbled further with his hands and lifted the

hinged door back. The opening was only about three feet square. Stark felt a moment's puzzlement that it hadn't been secured from below in some fashion. Then he understood that anybody using the escape route would likely be in too big of a rush to want to fool with having to unfasten a lock.

"Tunnel runs straight on. About a yard wide, as I recall," Silas confided in a whisper. He fumbled in his clothing and produced a stub of candle. "Take this."

"Much obliged, amigo." Stark accepted the candle. He hesitated, then shrugged out of the strap holding the Sporting Rifle. Its bulky length would probably just hinder his progress in the narrow passage. He kept the shotgun. "Hang onto it for me," he said, pressing the rifle on Silas. He hoped he wouldn't regret leaving the weapon behind.

Silas's knobby fist closed on the rifle. "I'll take care of it. Go with God."

"Yeah."

Stark slipped through the trapdoor. Here he was going blind into another hole in the ground, he mused grimly.

There was a sturdy ladder that descended about ten feet. Stark dropped the last half of the way, flexing his legs as he landed. He drew the Colt and crouched, listening, as Silas replaced the trapdoor. He didn't want to light the candle yet. It would make a fine target.

Darkness enfolded him. He could've kept his eyes closed for all the good they were going to do him in the Stygian gloom. This was how it must look in the grave, he thought fleetingly.

He stilled his breathing. Was he alone in the passage? Might Kincaid have it guarded? He heard nothing, smelled only dust and mold. The air itself had a stale, dead weight to it. No one had been down here for a long time.

He holstered the Colt and fumbled to get the candle lighted. Its flame revealed dirt walls to either side, and only blackness in front of him. Lifting the candle, he saw the ceiling was no more than a foot overhead.

Gun once more in hand, he paced carefully forward. Now that the candle was lit, a gunman waiting at the far end would have an easy shot. He offered up a silent prayer in the darkness.

The hundred yards seemed more like a couple of miles. The floor and walls remained featureless—nothing but packed dirt. Stark had the eerie notion he might keep walking through the unending darkness for eternity, forever doomed to seeing only a few feet ahead of him.

He had started to count his steps but soon lost track. Then, in front of him, he glimpsed something white on the floor. He slowed and felt his face pull taut at what the dancing flame revealed.

A human skeleton lay crumpled against the passage wall. The bony talons of the hands were curled deep in the dust of the floor. The skull was facing away from him. Stark imagined the empty eye sockets staring endlessly at the dirt wall inches in front of it. Yeah, like the grave, all right.

Who was he? At a glance there was no way to tell how he had died. Or why. The tattered clothing was white. Heavy sandals were on his feet, wrapped about with rags. One of the Mexican laborers Silas had seen? Stark wondered. Dead from the rigors of work in the winter months, or slain for some indiscretion and dumped here for convenience's sake?

He didn't know, and didn't have time to speculate. He was glad the skull wasn't facing him as he edged past. Whoever the dead man had been, he was undoubtedly another victim of the cruel power Lucius Kincaid wielded with invulnerability in his domain.

Twenty feet farther and the passage ended. Another ladder led up to a trapdoor. A small packet at its base proved to be a revolver and a candle with matches bound in oilskin. Kincaid was a careful man. If he had to use this escape route, he didn't plan to go unarmed or blinded by the gloom.

Stark knelt, and his hands moved with deft certainty. Straightening, he cast his eyes up at the waiting door. Above him the household would be stirring. He wished for a floor plan, but he'd just have to do without.

There was no benefit in cooling his heels down here. Stark extinguished the candle and stuffed it in his pocket. By feel, he clambered up the ladder, putting far to the back of his mind any thought of the skeleton lying below him in the darkness. He hoped his bones wouldn't be joining those of the dead man.

At the top of the ladder, he longed for a third hand. Clinging with his left to the splintery wood, he raised his right palm and cautiously tested the door. It lifted with only a little stiffness in the hinges. There was nothing but darkness over his head.

He went up another rung, easing the door back as far as he could with an outstretched arm, then letting it drop. It fell the rest of the way with only a muffled thump. Before the dust settled, Stark got his Colt in his hand and pulled himself smoothly up the rest of the way through the opening.

Poised on one knee, he waited for a span of seconds. The smells of foodstuffs and assorted durable goods told him Silas had been right. He had emerged in the cellar.

So far, the secret passage had been unguarded, which made plenty of sense. There wasn't any point in drawing attention to what was meant as a last-ditch escape route.

When he got the candle once more lighted, it revealed the expected jumble of materials to be found in the cellar of any large household. Wooden steps led up to a closed door. Stark mounted and pressed his ear against the panel. He heard nothing to alarm him. After a few moments he slid the blade of his bowie between the door and the jamb to flip the outside latch.

Cautiously, he pushed the panel back. A short flight of steep stone steps confronted him. He extinguished the candle and unlimbered the shotgun. Latching the basement door behind him, he trod swiftly up the stairs, pausing when his head was high enough to see what awaited him.

He was looking down a dim passage with a lighted doorway opening off it. No one was in sight. The scents of bacon and biscuits made his mouth water.

He advanced to the doorway and peered inside. As he'd guessed, it was a kitchen. Directly before him a weathered, dark-skinned woman was chopping peppers with a butcher knife on a massive wooden table. As his gaze fell on her, she lifted her head and looked directly at him.

The black eyes in her lined face opened wide, and she gasped. Stark pressed a warning finger to his lips and slipped through the door into the kitchen, hoping she was alone.

She was, he saw at a glance. And apparently she was responsible for doing all the cooking for Kincaid and his crew. Large skillets full of sausage and bacon sizzled and popped. An enormous black pot simmered over low flames in a huge fireplace. The temperature in the big room was enough to bring the sweat popping out immediately on his brow.

The woman was staring at him as if stricken. Stark berated himself furiously for his carelessness. What in blazes was he going to do with her?

"I won't harm you," he said. "But you must be silent. Understand?"

She managed a nod. The butcher knife in her hand seemed frozen in midstroke inches above a cleft pepper. She swallowed hard.

"Are you a *brujo,* a witch doctor, to walk through the walls and enter this place?" she stammered in English that bore the stamp of the Mexican border.

Up this close, her Spanish ancestry was evident. The thick, graying hair had once been lustrous and black. And the lines in her face were bred more of hard experience than of years.

"Just a man, *señora,*" he answered her politely. "And certainly not a *brujo.*"

She relaxed enough to lower the knife to the table. She made no effort to flee or cry out, but continued to regard him with piercing eyes. "Your are here for *el patrón,*" she said with sudden shrewdness. "You are the *muy hombre* they all fear, though they bluster and swagger about as if they do not." She turned her head and spat onto the floor. "Bah, they are all sorry dogs, like the man they serve!"

"*El patrón?*" Stark probed carefully. "Lucius Kincaid?"

"Yes, curse his black heart!" she hissed vehemently. "If I had the nerve, I would have served him rat poison in his food long before now! You have come for him, haven't you?"

Stark nodded. "He offered money to any man who would kill me. So far, none have been able to, though many have tried. Now I'll put a stop to it."

"By killing him?" she demanded eagerly.

"If I have to. What wrong has he done you, *señora*?"

She wagged her head back and forth. "Many wrongs. I was young and still good to look upon when I came here not so many years ago with my man. Now look at me! I am old and worn out, like a shoe."

"Where is your man?"

"He is dead. I am certain of it, though I have never seen his body. He simply disappeared one day after the house was finished. The *patrón* had him killed. I have always known this in my heart, but could never prove it. When I asked the *patrón*, he said Juan had run away, but I know he would not have left me like that. Somehow, he must've angered the *patrón*, as others have angered him. Once Juan was gone, the *patrón* kept me here to cook and . . . and to do other things for him. I have been here ever since. Now I just cook."

"Your man was one of the workers who helped build this house?"

She nodded sadly. "I came to cook for him and the others. Then he vanished."

Stark thought of a pitiful skeleton crumpled in darkness not too far from where she stood. He was sure he could explain some of the mystery of her Juan's disappearance. Lucius Kincaid, he reflected, left a powerful lot of enemies in his wake.

But now was not the time to reveal Juan's fate. "Can you help me, *señora*?" he asked softly.

Her hand tightened on the hilt of the knife until the veins and tendons in her gnarled wrist stood out in taut relief. "Yes, I can help you. What do you wish of me?"

"Where is Kincaid? Where can I find him?"

"He is waiting for breakfast in his den. With him is his bodyguard, and a man who is much like you, except he laughs too much and smiles too much, and has the eyes of a killer."

Gundance, Stark thought. He had been right to expect the manhunter to be awaiting him. "How do I get there from here?"

He listened as she told him. Then he asked more questions. There were two or three guards prowling about inside the house, but the den was on the ground floor, so he might manage to avoid them, if his luck held.

"Go quickly," she urged. "He will be expecting his breakfast."

"I'll give him something to chew on," Stark promised grimly, and slipped from the kitchen.

Chapter Fifteen

Stark and the patrolling guard saw each other at the same moment. The hallway was dim, and the hired gun wasn't really expecting trouble from deeper inside the house. But he cocked his head curiously as Stark lengthened his stride toward him.

"Any sign of him?" Stark demanded tersely as the distance between them narrowed. "The boss is on edge today."

The guard relaxed just a bit. He was wearing a pistol low at his side. "He's been on edge for days," he said with a snort, then peered more closely at Stark's shotgun-toting form. "Hey, don't reckon I've seen you before."

"Don't reckon you have," Stark agreed, and took one last lunging step forward to sweep the butt of the shotgun around in a short, savage arc.

The grasping hand of the hardcase slid limply from the butt of his pistol. His knees buckled as though a horse had been dropped on him, and he went down in a loose-limbed heap at Stark's feet.

Stark left him where he lay. Kincaid's den wasn't far now. Soundless in his Apache moccasins, he glided down the hallway. Halting at the massive double doors the cook had described, he glanced both ways. Satisfied, he dropped to one knee and put his eye to the keyhole.

It took a few seconds for the lavishly furnished room to come into focus. Almost immediately then he spotted a grotesque scarlet-robed figure near the bar, drink in hand. That was Kincaid. Nearby, propped against the wall like a carved figure, was the bodyguard with the battered face. Break, the cook had called him.

In another moment a lean form paced into view. There was no mistaking the catlike tread of Lance Trowbridge.

Stark straightened and pulled air into his lungs, once, twice. Gently he worked the lever of the shotgun, keeping it close to his body to muffle the sound. Then, shotgun leveled, finger on the trigger, he reached with his left hand to turn one ornate knob. As the door opened, he slid through and heeled it shut behind him. He was inside, covering all three of them, before they even fully realized he was in the room.

Gundance turned swiftly and caught himself, poised to draw, as he took in the shotgun. The bodyguard levered himself away from the wall, fists clenched. The half-filled glass dropped from Kincaid's hand. It fell almost soundlessly onto the Navajo rug. The whiskey spread in a dark stain. Other than that, the Eastern millionaire didn't move.

''Stark,'' he breathed.

''Yeah,'' Stark drawled. ''Gundance must've warned you I'd be coming, and that no price on my head was going to stop me. Should've taken his warning to heart. You put a bounty on the wrong man, Kincaid. Now I'm here to collect a bounty of my own. It cancels yours out.''

''Not so fast, Peacemaker,'' Lance Trowbridge said at last with a familiar, easy grin. ''You knew I'd be here, didn't you?''

''It figured,'' Stark said. ''Where else would a good hunter be but waiting for his prey?''

Trowbridge chuckled. ''Just like I told Kincaid. I called it, sure enough.'' He relaxed out of his fighting stance. He still looked cool and sure of himself and mighty dangerous, Stark thought. ''Before you deal with Kincaid, we got some business between us, Stark.''

''You aim to try your hand at collecting the bounty?''

''Nope.'' The grin flashed. ''I aim to collect it. Prove who's the better man.''

Stark moved the barrel of the shotgun just a hair. ''Already been proved,'' he opined. ''You're under the gun. That settles who's better. You never had a chance. I could've cut you down the second I walked through the door.''

''But you didn't.'' Trowbridge purred. ''Because that wouldn't prove a thing. We're both alike, you and me. Come right down to it, we both have to know who's best.''

Trowbridge was right, Stark acknowledged the truth of what was deep in that part of himself that made him a man in his own estimate. It had always been building to this between him and Gundance. Stark was a professional. He didn't favor killing when it wasn't needful, and he didn't favor giving a foe an even break out of any amateur's notion of fair play. He had nothing to prove. He was good at what he did, maybe the best.

But Lance Trowbridge was the one man living who he fancied just might be better. And not knowing, taking him down without giving him a chance, would ever after eat at Stark like an ulcer in his gut. As Trowbridge said, he had to know which of them was better. Even if it killed him, he had to know.

And it just might kill him. He swept his gaze over Kincaid and the threatening Break. Trowbridge wasn't the only enemy he had to worry about.

The manhunter caught the quick movement of his eyes. Without looking, he tossed a command over his shoulder. "Both of you stay out of this, or I'll kill you myself." His own gaze, avid and expectant, rested on Stark. "Satisfied?"

Slowly Stark lowered the shotgun and leaned it against the wall beside the doors. He stepped carefully clear. A tingling crept over his muscles. All of his senses seemed heightened. He figured Gundance was feeling the same thing.

"How much?" he asked. "You're not doing this for any five thousand dollars."

Trowbridge smirked. "Why, I calculated your sorry hide to be worth at least twice that. Kincaid agreed, providing I'd give him a guarantee."

"That's still not enough," Stark said. He stood with his gun hand hovering above and a little in front of his holstered Colt.

Trowbridge was straight as a fence post. His arms were at his sides, fingers flexed. His eyes bore a distracted look, as though he was listening to some distant sound. His easygoing grin had turned fixed and hard.

"Reckon now's the time to earn your pay," Stark allowed.

"I reckon." Gundance cocked his head. "Would you listen to that?" he said unexpectedly. "It's louder than I've ever heard it."

Stark didn't know what in blazes he was talking about. Trowbridge didn't give him a chance to wonder. Not waiting for Stark's move, he drew with a twitch of his hand.

There was a frozen moment when Stark knew he was beaten, knew of a certainty that Gundance had shaded him. Then his own hand, moving outside of his will, far beyond his conscious thought or control, brought the .45 clear of leather in a smooth circular sweep faster—*faster*—that Trowbridge's gun was rising. The Colt bucked and roared in Stark's hand while Gundance's hammer was still falling.

The two shots rang out almost, but not quite, together. By the smallest fraction of a second, Stark's shot came first. Trowbridge was rocked backward. His jaw dropped in surprise as Stark felt heat sear past his side. Trowbridge caught himself. His legs stiffened with the strength of his determination, and his Colt came levering up once more.

"Dance," Stark said, and shot him again.

Still on his feet, Trowbridge's body jerked. He gave one last wondering shake of his head before he fell. He shot the floor on his way down. Gundance was dead.

"Now we both know," Stark murmured.

He heard the pound of heavy feet, glimpsed the stunningly fast motion of the bodyguard. He never would've thought the big man could move so quickly. He tried to duck and swivel about. But he was too slow, and maybe Break was the best of them all.

One sledging fist came in like a runaway ore car and crashed into the side of his head. He slewed about under the impact. His gun flew from his hand. A roaring sound exploded in his ears.

He saw another fist coming. Over Break's heavy shoulder he had a fleeting view of Kincaid's face alight with an evil glee. In giving Kincaid his chance, he realized, he just might've lost his own to get out of this alive.

"It's an absolute fortress!" Prudence McKay exclaimed softly, gazing down into the vale at the compound below. "And there are guards everywhere!"

Mounted beside her, Heck Thomas worked his jaws as though he was literally chewing over the situation. At last he looked past Prudence and drawled, "What do you think, Stand?"

Positioned on her other side, Garner stilled his big gelding. He'd stuck by Prudence like a cockleburr for most of the night's ride. She suspected Heck had told him to keep an eye on her. She also suspected he'd been happy to oblige. Sometimes his leg had brushed hers as they rode. She'd done her best to disregard his distracting male presence, but she'd been acutely aware of it just the same.

Now, in the early-morning sunlight, save for a faint stubble on his strong jaw, he didn't look any the worse for wear. She wondered if she could say the same of herself. Stand sure didn't seem to mind looking her over. She felt tired and sore and a little angry at James

Stark. But her overriding concern for his well-being made her glance sharply at the younger deputy, impatient for his reply to his superior's question.

"We rode all night just to get here that much sooner," Garner opined at last. "No point in wasting time now. Hit fast and hard, run roughshod over those guards, and then go in and get our man."

He looked eager for trouble and quite capable of handling it, Prudence reflected.

So far, they'd met up with no serious resistance. Faced with the options of pulling up stakes or getting taken into custody by hard-eyed U.S. Deputies, the outriders they'd encountered, to a man, had chosen to hit the trail. There had been no further trace of any of them.

Where was James? Prudence found herself questioning over and over. Was it possible he had made it through the cordon of outriders and reached this place ahead of them? Surely not, she concluded doubtfully. She gnawed on a thumbnail as she studied the layout below. If he was here, where *was* he? What sort of danger was he in? Fear for him made her tremble suddenly in the saddle. Thankfully, if any of the posse members saw this evidence of her distress, they gave no sign.

Heck propped his forearms thoughtfully on his saddle horn. "Don't figure we'll play it your way, just yet, Stand," he advised without looking at his subordinate. "Could be those hired guns down yonder won't want to tangle with a bunch of U.S. Deputies. We'll just mosey in kind of peacefullike and give them that choice, leastways. No profit in wasting lead and lives if it ain't absolutely needful."

He broke off and swiveled his head sharply to stare

down the valley, as though something had caught his eye. Prudence followed his gaze, but saw only waves of rippling grass stretching the length of the valley.

Heck grunted and shook his head. "Must be starting to see things," he muttered. He looked directly at Prudence. "You stay here."

Automatically she opened her mouth, but his unyielding expression stilled her words. He was right, she knew. Granted, she could ride and even shoot if the need arose. But in the type of battle that might await them down below, she would only be in the way of these professional manhunters. She couldn't stand the thought of one of them taking a bullet trying to protect her.

Reluctantly she held her palomino in as the posse wended its way down out of the hills. They carried their saddle guns unsheathed, butts resting against their legs. The image of knights and their lances came to her mind. Stand Garner turned and gave her a jaunty wave. She realized she was chewing at her thumbnail again and forced her hand resolutely to her thigh. Suddenly she felt very much alone and vulnerable.

The posse members reached the valley floor, and a handful of riders came galloping out to meet them, kicking up a cloud of dust as they did. Some sort of conference ensued, with Heck doing most of the talking. One of the guards turned abruptly and took off down the valley like he wasn't coming back. The others fell in ahead of the posse almost as though they were cattle being herded.

Then, only faintly audible, but clearly identifiable, came the sounds of gunshots from the big stone house.

Heck and his men heard them. They pulled up

sharply. Some of the guards they'd been herding swung their mounts about to face them. Words were exchanged. The guards were clearly blocking them from proceeding to the house.

Leaning tensely forward in her saddle, Prudence couldn't see what started it, but suddenly gunfire erupted from both parties. Muzzle flames and powder smoke spurted. She was too far away to make out details, but she heard the distinctive boom of Heck's sawed-off shotgun.

Within a handful of seconds the guards were sprawling from their mounts. One of the horses streaked away, its rider reeling in the saddle. None of the lawmen had gone down, Prudence saw with relief.

Heck waved an arm toward the house and shouted a command. Spreading out in a wide line, the deputies charged. Stand was getting his way, after all. Prudence spotted him, reins in his teeth, wielding a rifle in one hand and a six-gun in the other. Shots from the rallying guards in front of the house began to answer.

Prudence could stand it no longer. She pulled the .32 from her holster, pounded her heels against the palomino's ribs, and went tearing down the hill in the wake of the posse.

Chapter Sixteen

Stark managed to stay on his feet after Break's first punishing blow. Desperately he tried to block the follow-up punch. His own forearm was pounded back against his skull as it took the brunt of the impact. Hands clenched, arms bent in front of his face and chest, he tried to weather the storm of fists that followed. Break's hard knuckles battered at his guard. He hunched his shoulders, then gasped as Break whipped a wicked left down to his side.

Stark had fought in the ring; he could recognize another old hand at the brutal trade. But he had also trained in the demanding art of savate, which combined European pugilism with French-style foot fighting. Given time, he might've beaten Break in the ring, even allowing for that first sucker punch.

But he didn't have time. Kincaid could summon reinforcements at his whim. Thankfully, though, for the moment he seemed eager to watch his bruiser dish out punishment.

And Break was doing just that, switching from swinging blows to straight driving punches with no way to tell what was coming next. If Stark couldn't withstand his assault and somehow turn the tables, he sensed

Break's unrelenting fists could kill him just as dead as Trowbridge's gun.

Absorbing the pounding on his forearms, he shifted weight onto his left foot, leaned back, and drove the flat of his right foot against Break's ankle. He wished for his hard-soled riding boots. But even in a moccasin, the kick jammed Break's leg. He faltered, and Stark sent a solid uppercut tearing up to his jaw, before ducking clear of his fists at last.

Break grinned, realizing he might be in for a fight. Plainly, he relished it. His own guard was up. Stark was out of range of his fists, but Break wasn't out of range of Stark's feet. Pivoting on his anchor leg, Stark whipped a kick around at his opponent. He aimed not for the head or for the body, but for the bent elbow of Break's arm. The funny bone.

The ball of Stark's foot drove against the outside of Break's elbow, then snapped away. Break winced, surprised. Delivered with the full leverage and muscle of Stark's leg, the impact had been even harder than a fist. There'd be a tingling in Break's elbow now. Snarling, he thrust out a straight punch with his other arm. It fell short. In the half-instant his arm was at full extension, Stark leaned sideward and snapped the edge of his foot up to the vulnerable armpit. Break jerked his arm back, pressing it tight against his body for a moment to let the pain pass.

Stark had realized that he'd have a hard time getting past the boxer's guard. Unless he destroyed it. Fast and hard, dancing and gliding just out of reach of Break's stabbing, sweeping fists, Stark threw his high savate kicks. He kept aiming at key targets on Break's lifted arms: wrist, elbow, shoulder, armpit, bicep. Not all of them landed, but plenty did.

"Get him, you stupid ox!" Kincaid screamed. "What's wrong with you? You're not even trying to hit him!"

What was wrong with Break was that his arms were no longer working like they were supposed to. He was having more and more trouble even holding them up, much less throwing punches with them. His ring-scarred face was a mask of pain and rage. And the beginnings of fear.

Then the ball of Stark's left foot powered against his shoulder, shaking his whole big frame and smashing that shoulder jarringly into his cheek. His arms sagged ever further. Another few moments, and they'd be all but useless.

Stark saw Kincaid whirl away from the fight to stare toward the curtained windows. Faintly, over the roaring still in his head, he fancied he heard shots.

Break lashed out clumsily. Stark stepped clear to deliver another kick. As his foot left the floor, commotion erupted outside the house. Now there was no doubt that he heard gunfire. Voices were raised in excited yells.

"U.S. Marshals!" a man's strident tones carried clearly.

Stark's kick misfired. He hopped to regain his balance. Break lurched past him, carried by the force of his missed swing. Kincaid spun away from the window. One hand disappeared into the opposite sleeve of his voluminous gown. It reappeared with a gleaming sliver of steel, which he flung backhanded. A gambler's dirk, it flew straight for Stark's chest.

Stark twisted aside, and the wicked little weapon shot past with inches to spare. Kincaid lumbered frantically for the doors in a wild dash. Stark sprang to intercept him, and, almost too late, remembered Break.

The prizefighter's arms had been battered to near uselessness, but he wasn't out of the fight yet. He lowered his bullet head and charged. His hard skull, Stark understood, could be even more dangerous than his fists if it ever connected solidly.

He wheeled outside of Break's rush. Kincaid yanked open the doors and disappeared into the hallway. Stark had no chance to go after him. Break came about and charged again, for all the world like one of the bull buffalo from Silas's old days on the prairie.

Stark forgot about Kincaid for the moment. He had to, if he figured to get out of here alive. He sidestepped past Gundance's sprawled body to have room. As Break came hurtling toward him, he swept his stiffened leg around in a circular movement. His timing had to be perfect, or he'd be overrun and trampled by Break's charge.

The arc of his sweeping leg intercepted the path of Break's lowered head like a swinging wagon tongue. Stark felt the impact of foot against skull all the way up to his hip socket. The force of it whirled him halfway about. Stunned, Break lurched to a halt, head hanging.

Stark completed his spin. Coming out of it, he planted the aching foot he'd used to club Break, and jacked his other leg high. Straight down he brought it, like swinging a sledge. The heel of his foot smashed against the nape of Break's offered neck and hammered him face-first onto the floor in a motionless pile.

Stark staggered, then caught his balance. His breath was coming in great gasps. The uproar still sounded from the front of the house. The coming of the federal lawmen must've prevented Kincaid's guards from investigating the gunshots he and Trowbridge had exchanged. He owed a debt of thanks to whoever was responsible for their arrival.

But it was a debt that would have to wait. Retrieving his Colt from the floor, he snatched up the shotgun and bolted from the room. With the lawmen closing in, he knew where Kincaid was headed. He'd make for the secret tunnel, with notions of holing up there until night, or trying to reach the barn and get a horse. Regardless, he bid fair to make his escape if things broke his way.

Stark glimpsed the crimson-clad bulk just disappearing around a corner at the end of the hall. Face grim, he stalked after him. From behind came the muffled sounds of the gun battle going on. Somewhere a woman screamed. Stark remembered the blond he'd seen in a window. Kincaid's men weren't of the ilk to stand up to a determined assault by U.S. lawmen. They'd fold soon enough.

Tucking the shotgun under one arm, Stark reloaded the Colt by feel as he walked. He kept his gaze ahead of him, alert for any other tricks from Kincaid. The fat man had already proved himself to be dangerous even without bodyguards and hired guns.

Past the kitchen Stark strode, sparing only a glance inside. The cook was nowhere in sight.

Kincaid had been sharp enough to pull the cellar door shut so as not to leave evidence of his passing. Stark threw it open and went·in low, shotgun sweeping the darkened chamber. Nothing moved in the gloom. A haze of dust hanging in the air betrayed someone's recent presence.

Warily Stark descended the steps and crossed to the trapdoor. He yanked it up and stepped back. No gunfire stabbed up to meet him out of the darkness. He fancied a faint gleam shone from below.

Setting the shotgun aside, he palmed the Colt and went through the trapdoor. His boot touched a ladder rung only once to slow his drop. He twisted his body so he was facing down the passage when he landed with flexed knees.

The tunnel was strangely bright. Silhouetted partway down its length, just passing the white blur of the skeleton, Kincaid was lumbering along at a good clip. His bulky frame almost filled the passageway.

Stark stood with the Colt in his fist dangling at his side. "Kincaid!" he shouted. He didn't raise the .45.

Kincaid whirled about before the first echoes had finished. Stark saw him fling his arm up, saw the glint of metal in his fist.

"Don't fire that gun!" Stark shouted.

The explosion flared blindingly bright in the gloom. Its echoes scattered the lingering reverberations of Stark's shouts. Kincaid cried out and toppled backward. Stark could've sworn the floor of the tunnel vibrated with the impact of his fall.

Deliberately he paced forward, Colt still hanging loosely in his grip. He stopped and stood over Kincaid's lifeless form. The Eastern millionaire had fallen just past all that was left of the cook's husband.

Motion down the passageway brought Stark's head

and gun up with simultaneous jerks. He relaxed as he recognized the small wiry figure of Silas. Stark's big repeating rifle was held competently in his fists. The dim illumination in the tunnel came from the outside entrance.

"Started to leave, then figured I might ought to wait for you," the old man explained. He broke off as he got a good look at Kincaid's sprawled bulk and the peeled-back barrel of the revolver in his pudgy fist. "Heaven's sake, what happened to him?"

"His pistol blew up in his hand when he tried to use it. The barrel was plugged with dirt. I tried to warn him, but he wasn't much good at listening to warnings."

Silas stared at him hard. "You do the plugging?"

Stark hitched his shoulders. "He'd left a pistol down here in case he ever needed to take this route to escape. I didn't figure on taking a chance he might end up using it on me."

"Died by his own hand, you might say."

"Yeah, you might."

"He'd had it coming for a long time." Silas shook himself like a buffalo shaking off dust from a wallow. He proffered the Sporting Rifle to Stark. "Told you I'd take care of it."

"Obliged."

"Reckon it's over now. Don't guess I'll be coming back to this place much."

"Look me up if you're ever in Guthrie."

Silas snorted. "Not likely. But I'll still be out here when civilization starts closing in on you."

"I'll remember that. Keep your powder dry."

"I'll do it." Silas paused as he started to turn away.

''You better go back and square things with them law dogs. I saw them coming in. Darnedest thing.''

''What's that?''

''There was a woman riding with them. Leastways, she came tearing in on their tail.''

''A woman?'' Stark demanded with an unsettling premonition.

Silas nodded firmly. ''For a fact. Pretty little dark-haired thing, far as I could tell.''

Stark scowled. He could make a good guess as to whom he owed that debt of thanks.

Chapter Seventeen

"It was a fool thing to do!" Stark insisted, "putting your life in danger that way!"

"You put yours in danger by coming after Kincaid," Prudence pointed out tartly.

She'd found time to freshen up after the fracas, Stark had noted. Even with her hazel eyes sparking fire, she looked mighty appealing to him. "My life was already in danger," he answered her a little belatedly. "Folks were trying to kill me right and left."

"Besides," she continued as if he hadn't spoken, "I was never at any real risk. The shooting was almost over before I got very close."

Stark snorted derisively, and she had the grace to look a bit contrite for such a fool statement. He swung his gaze about the tastefully furnished parlor off the main hallway of the prairie fortress. He could hear the muted sounds of Heck Thomas and his men tying up the loose ends left by their assault.

"You should've listened to me back in Guthrie when I told you the law could handle things," Prudence recovered her aplomb enough to point out. "If you had, none of this would've happened. I came out here to help you."

"I didn't need any help!"

Prudence's eyes widened infuriatingly. "You were in here taking on Kincaid and his two killers, one of whom, by your own admission, was your equal, if not your superior—"

"He found out different, didn't he?" Stark interjected smugly.

Prudence's lips curled scornfully. "And there was an army of hired guns to back them up. You didn't need any help?"

Stark's grace didn't match hers. "I could've handled it."

Prudence's eyes went even wider. "How, if I may ask?"

It was sure hard for him to look down at her, even though she was so tiny, Stark thought. "I would've taken Kincaid hostage, forced his gun hands to back down, then ridden out of here with him," he asserted.

"And then what? Killed him?" She flashed with sudden anger. "Like you killed who knows how many other men on your way here?"

"I passed over a few of them," Stark said with a growl, "for now."

He seemed to have scored some sort of point, for she bit her lower lip with small white teeth.

"And even if the law could've handled it," he went on roughly, "there was no need for you to come traipsing after me, traveling with six men out on the prairie at night!"

Prudence's pretty face went white, and her eyes narrowed dangerously. Stark resisted the impulse to retreat a couple of steps.

"I'll have you know they were all perfect gentlemen!" she spit the words like bullets.

"Even that big galoot, Garner? I saw him making eyes at you," Stark said. He'd been sure to learn the fellow's name. "You didn't seem to mind none!"

Prudence went from dead white to bright scarlet in an instant. But she wasn't backing down either. "And if I didn't mind, what business is it of yours?" she shot back. "Go ahead! Tell me!" She was trembling, whether with rage or expectancy, he didn't know.

"None, I reckon," he said bitterly.

She drew in her breath abruptly. Her eyelids fluttered. She turned sharply away. "All right." Her voice was oddly muffled. "I'm sorry for worrying about you. I'm sorry for trying to help you. I'm sorry for coming after you. I'm sorry for . . . for caring about you!"

She made a sound like a stifled sob and fled the room. Stark heard her rapidly departing footfalls.

Fuming, he paced the confines of the parlor like it was a cell. What had he come within a hairbreadth of telling her just then? he wondered fiercely. How should he have answered her question? What had she expected—or wanted—him to admit?

Suddenly he wheeled and strode from the room. Outside in the hallway, a deputy named Murphy looked as if he was about to speak, then quickly changed his mind. Stark barely noticed.

He came out onto the veranda, his eyes sweeping back and forth. At the far end of the long porch Prudence was engaged in converstaion with a man who stood within arm's length of her. Stark recognized Deputy Stand Garner. His heavy-shouldered figure dwarfed Prudence's petite shape.

Stark went toward them, his stride lengthening. Prudence was assuring Garner she was all right. At the last moment Garner sensed his coming, and started to turn his head. Stark shouldered roughly in front of the bigger man and looked down at Prudence. He heard Garner's offended grunt.

"You ready to go home?" Stark asked gruffly.

Prudence gazed searchingly up into his face. Her eyes were very bright. "Yes," she said, "I think I am. If you'll excuse us, Deputy."

She drew Stark away and tucked her arm possessively through his.